GH

Above the hills, the light shimmered and moved, shapes forming wraith-like in the pale air. Graves crossed himself, suddenly remembering the stories his mother had told him of guppies and nightwalkers. He had seen mirages before, but never so clear, never so large across the sky.

The light shifted, outlining the mirage as clearly as though the riders were only a mile or so distant. They were Comanches, paint distinct upon faces and chests. War paint. They carried rifles and the traditional lances of the horse warriors. And from the upraised lances hung long bunches of hair that the Indians waved and flourished, shouting soundless cries.

'Madre de Dios!' Paco gasped, kissing the rosary hung around his neck.

The others gaped, the Mexicans mumbling fervent prayers, the halfbreeds crossing themselves or making the two-fingered gesture that fends off evil spirits.

Graves felt the sweat washing his back turn suddenly cold, and shivered, gritting his teeth. He reined in, turning in his saddle. 'It ain't nothin'! Just a goddam mirage . . .'

Also in the BREED series and available from Sphere Books

THE LONELY HUNT

THE SILENT KILL

Breed
Cry For Vengeance

JAMES A. MUIR

SPHERE BOOKS LIMITED
30/32 Gray's Inn Road, London WC1X 8JL

First published in Great Britain
by Sphere Books Ltd 1977

TRADE MARK

Set in Intertype Plantin

Printed in Great Britain by
C. Nicholls & Company Ltd
The Philips Park Press, Manchester

For Gumdrop

CHAPTER ONE

Heat, like a shroud, lay over the Staked Plains. It blistered out of a sky so bright a man's eyes hurt from looking at it. The sandy ground sent back answering waves, so that the land shimmered, seeming to writhe and undulate like a wriggling snake. But no snakes showed: like the other inhabitants of the desert, they were not so foolish as to venture into the baking sunlight. High above, riding the thermals like black exclamation marks cut into the blue-white sky, hung vultures. It was cooler at that height, but not by much.

The desert was still, biding its time, waiting for the cool of evening. Nothing moved.

Except the men.

Men are foolish; or obstinate: it depends on the viewpoint. They go places the lesser creatures are sensible enough to leave well alone. They travel at times when any intelligent beast seeks shelter and rest. They ignore the basic rules that govern the balance of nature. They refuse to admit their smallness on the scales of the world.

These particular men were accustomed to heat, and spurred by greed. Four of them were Mexicans, using their wide-brimmed sombreros to puddle shadow over faces and hands. Three were halfbreeds, their dark, thick-set features emphasising their mixed parentage. One was a negro. All eight rode solid, reliable-looking horses with carbines sheathed along the saddles and more hardwear showing around their belts. They herded a string of sixteen mules, each one carrying a canvas-wrapped bundle on its swaying, sweating back. The movement, gentle though it was, for they moved slowly in the heat, caused the bundles to clink faintly, the rattle of metal on metal.

A mile away on the far side of a low bluff, a second group

of men hunkered in the shade of some big saguaros. They were mostly dressed in breech clouts and paint, though a few wore fine buckskin shirts. Their hair was uniformly black and long, their faces broad, with heavy noses and calm, cold eyes. They were Comanches.

To one side of the saguaros stood a group of fifteen mustangs, watched over by the two youngest warriors. The others lay or squatted, in silence or low-voiced conversation. They carried lances and bows and they were waiting for the riders.

The riders were Comancheros.

As they pushed through the heat haze a Comanche stretched out on the crest of the bluff let his eyes wander slowly over the flatlands. He caught a sight of the cavalcade and turned, calling a gutteral warning down the slope. The Indians resting below glanced up, one rising to his feet. He was tall for a Comanche, his broad chest covered with a painted quill bib, streaks of black and red dye banding his face. Plaited into his hair were three eagle feathers. He was called Iron Knife and he led the warriors.

The leader of the Comancheros had been christened Samuel Graves. The surname was that of the planter who had owned him; the other, his father's name. His men called him *El Negro* because of his coal-black skin. He had escaped the plantation when he was sixteen and stowed away on a Mississippi river boat that took him down to New Orleans. After that he had worked and hidden and run until he ended up in Mexico. By then he was big enough that most men thought twice about commenting on the colour of his skin, and good enough with gun or knife to settle any who did comment. He had worked around the border for a few years, drifting until he met Jaime Sanchez and they set up together as Indian traders. Guns and liquor offered a higher profit margin than legal trading, and soon El Negro was one of the wealthiest Comancheros in the territory.

His latest venture promised to make him wealthier still.

Iron Knife watched the riders coming, picking out the darker tint of Graves' skin from the swarthy tones of his companions. It was unlikely that anyone else would venture this deep into Comanche territory, but the Indian was careful by nature, so he made no move until he was absolutely sure. Then he moved back down the slope, signalling to his men.

The Comanches mounted their ponies, falling into line behind Iron Knife as he rode towards the agreed meeting place.

Almost too high up to be seen, a vulture picked out the movement and spiralled lower, watching the ground. It was an old vulture and well-fed: long ago it had learned that groups of men often meant easy pickings.

The Comanches rode slowly, taking care to let the Comancheros arrive first. Then they came forward, silent as Graves' called out a greeting. The traders had dismounted and Iron Knife, with two others, followed suit; the remaining Indians spread in a semi-circle around the group.

'*Hola,*' said El Negro. '*Que va?*'

'*Bien.*' Iron Knife replied in Spanish, the lingua franca of the South West.

Cigars were handed out and the three Indians squatted, puffing on the aromatic black tobacco. Then, the rituals of greetings dispensed with, they settled down to business.

Graves motioned to one of the halfbreeds and a mule was brought forward. The negro rose to his feet and tugged on the drawstring holding the pack secure. The canvas fell away and the mule skittered sideways as rifles clattered to the ground. Most were single-shot Spencers, relics of the Civil War, but amongst the pile of weapons Iron Knife could see lever-action Henrys and early-model Winchesters. He grunted his appreciation. Graves nodded and reached for a gun packed separately to the rest. It was a .44-40 Winchester carbine, in better condition than the others. He handed it to the Comanche.

Iron Knife checked over the gun, working the lever and dropping the hammer on the empty chamber until he was satisfied of its condition. Graves handed him shells, and the Indian loaded, sighted out into the desert and began to fire. Unused to the handling of a Winchester, he fired slowly, his shots erratic, but his face split in a savage smile while his braves whooped their appreciation.

Graves waited until his customer was satisfied, then gestured at the string of pack animals.

'There are one hundred rifles there, Iron Knife, and fifty pistols.'

'How many of the fast-fire guns?' interrupted the Indian.

'Twenty-five,' replied Graves, easily. 'That was all I could get. They're harder to come by than the others.'

Iron Knife grunted: 'Bullets?'

'Three loads. The other mules carry powder and shot for the slow-fire rifles.'

'Good.' Iron Knife looked pleased. 'You do well, Black One.'

'Yeah,' said the negro, 'an' I can get more. If you got the gold.'

The Comanche called something in his own language and four warriors walked their ponies forward. They each carried two heavy-looking sacks which they let fall to the ground. Iron Knife kicked one with a moccasined toe.

'Open it.'

Graves knelt, cutting through the rawhide thong holding a sack closed. Dull yellow gold dust glinted briefly in the sun, and he smiled, re-fastening the sack.

'I ain't about to ask where you got it,' he grinned, 'but it's a deal.'

'You get more guns?' Iron Knife asked.

'Sure.' El Negro watched his men stow the sacks onto the pack saddle of a mule. 'You bring more gold; you get more guns.'

'How long?' The question was guttural, urgent.

Graves shrugged. 'Maybe two moons. Come here then.'

'We come,' nodded the Indian. 'Get the guns that fire fast.'

'I'll do my best,' said Graves, 'but I ain't makin' no guarantees.'

Iron Knife studied the smiling black face for a moment, then, Indian-fashion when a conversation is ended, he spun abruptly on his heel and walked away. Graves watched him spring onto the pad saddle of a pinto mustang, yank his war lance from the ground and ride away. The other Comanches herded the mules together in a tight group and used their lances to goad the animals to a fast canter. After a while they were gone into the heat mist.

'Let's get the hell outta here,' shouted Graves, climbing into his own saddle. 'John Bear, you take the mule.'

The halfbreed grabbed the lead rein and hauled the mule behind him. As much as his impassive face could show emotion it looked as though he was pleased to be riding out.

Graves rode in silence, aware of a prickling along his spine that had nothing to do with the heat. He was accustomed to trading with the Comanches, and knew that the Indians were too intelligent to risk cutting off the supply of goods he brought them. But there was something about this new deal that made him uneasy. The tribes had shown no sign of starting a new war, but they were amassing more guns than ever before, and that made the tight, black curls covering his scalp tingle nervously.

His men seemed to share the feeling.

Paco, the oldest of the Mexicans, spurred his stallion alongside the negro's mount, a worried expression showing through the drooping moustache that obscured his lower face.

'What you think, *jefe*? What's old Iron Knife up to?'

'Don't rightly know,' answered Graves. 'He's pickin' up dust from somewhere, an' he's sure as hell stockin' up on guns. Maybe he's plannin' a war.'

'Which might be a bad thing,' murmured Paco.

'How's that?' Graves wondered if the Mexican had the same doubts he felt. 'We got paid, didn't we?'

'Si,' grunted Paco, glancing quizzically at the black man, 'but when he has all the guns he wants; what then?'

'You mean he could turn nasty?' Graves said thoughtfully. 'Decide that maybe he don't need us anymore?'

Pacco nodded: '*Si.*'

'He'll still want ammunition. An' most o' them single shots are gonna fall apart after they been fired a coupla times.'

'But the repeaters we sell them,' said Paco softly, 'they will last. And if Iron Knife starts a new war, the territory will sprout men like the Spring grass.'

'Yeah.' The negro looked at Paco with new respect. 'I get yore drift. A war means soldiers. If Iron Knife cuts loose like Roman Nose did up in Kansas, the whole o' Texas will be crawlin' with bluecoats and Rangers. That could shut the border off tighter'n a whore at a Quaker picnic. An' that's bad fer business.'

He lapsed into moody silence and Paco said no more, leaving El Negro to his own thoughts as they headed south.

The sun remained hot as ever, prompting men to slump wordlessly in their saddles, salt sweat caking over their faces. Far away, in the direction of Mexico, a range of hills butted from the flat terrain, bleached white by wind and sun so that they reflected light back into the eyes of a watcher. Samuel Graves glanced towards them, and moved his gaze away as the blinding dazzle brought tears with its intensity. Then he looked back and his jaw dropped, his mouth opening in surprise.

Above the hills, the light shimmered and moved, shapes forming wraith-like in the pale air. Graves crossed himself, suddenly remembering the stories his mother had told him of guppies and nightwalkers. He had seen mirages before, but never so clear, never so large across the sky.

The light shifted, outlining the mirage as clearly as though the riders were only a mile or so distant. They were Comanches, paint distinct upon faces and chests. War paint. They carried rifles and the traditional lances of the horse warriors. And from the upraised lances hung long bunches of hair that the Indians waved and flourished, shouting soundless cries.

'*Madre de Dios!*' Paco gasped, kissing the rosary hung around his neck.

The others gasped, the Mexicans mumbling fervent prayers, the halfbreeds crossing themselves or making the two-fingered gesture that fends off evil spirits.

Graves felt the sweat washing his back turn suddenly cold, and shivered, gritting his teeth.

He reined in, turning in his saddle.

'It ain't nothin'! Just a goddam mirage. Some bucks been out on the prod an' got theirselves a few scalps. That's all, dammit!'

'I hope so, muttered Paco, 'but strange that it should show just now, and so clear.'

'It ain't nothin',' Graves repeated. 'Nothin'.'

After that, the Comancheros grouped closer together and rode with one hand resting close to the carbines sheathed in their saddles. John Bear drew into the centre of the group, leading the pack mule so that it was surrounded by his companions.

They rode in silence, scanning the plains with more than their usual caution, each man anxious to find a safe camp where they could fort up for the night.

They reached a crumbled mesa around dusk. The flat-topped outcrop had been eroded close to the ground by wind and rain, tumbled boulders surrounding its flanks, and one side smoothed away to a kind of ramp. Graves called a halt and they made camp with the mesa at their backs and fallen rock to the front and sides. Look-out duties were assigned, and the first guard climbed the slope to the tabletop, hunkering down with his eyes on the desert as the air turned cold and the moon showed across the badlands.

Below, his companions built a fire, taking care to site it close to the rock wall, where it would be invisible beyond a few yards.

They set coffee to boil and meat to roast, and someone produced a bottle of tequila. It made them feel a little better.

Almost five hundred miles away in south-east Texas the brig *Elizabeth James* swung against her anchor chains in Galveston harbour. Rowboats ferried the passengers ashore, dumping them with their baggage on the lamplit wharf. Only five people disembarked, a married couple, an elderly widow, and two men. The men were well-dressed, but carried little in the way of luggage. One was tall, dark-haired, with green eyes that stayed cold even when he smiled. The other was shorter, a blond man with a lazy Southern drawl and a curiously high-pitched laugh, almost girlish in its giggling intensity. They both wore Colt .45 revolvers which had stayed with them throughout the sea passage.

The blond man was called Jude Christie. The other was Nolan; he had never offered a first name.

CHAPTER TWO

'Thar y'go, Mr. Gunn. That'll see you clear through to San Antone an' Houston. You wanna cut south to Galveston, you can pick up a rig an' be paddlin' on the Gulf afore you can say "William Travis".'

The ticket clerk thrust a yard-long stretch of paper through the pigeon hole cut into the depot window and grinned nervously at the passenger. The man was young and had offered no reason for the clerk's nervousness, but Ben Weaver had been manning the Brandon's Hole line-stop for too long that he couldn't recognise a hardcase when he saw one. And if he ever had, there was one facing him now.

Outwardly, there was nothing to set the man apart from the other drifters who purchased tickets from time to time, except maybe the Apache-style moccasins he wore, laced to knee height, with the dark leather haft of a knife sticking up from the right leg. His shirt was white – more or less – and looked reasonably clean, if well worn. His pants were of buckskin, common enough in the South West, as was the wide-brimmed black hat he wore. The Colt holstered snug on his right hip and the broad-bladed bowie knife hung on the left were standard equipment. It was the eyes that made Weaver jumpy. They were very blue, and very cold, and they seemed to take in everything around in one casual glance. Something about the man made the clerk think of the Apaches he had seen when he was scouting for the Army. His face was wide-boned, the nose broad, slightly flattened above the straight line of his full-lipped mouth; a face that might have belonged to an Indian. But his hair, hanging close to his shoulders was a sun-bleached blond colour that no Apache had ever owned.

Weaver had watched him walk in to Brandon's Hole with a

saddle hoisted on his back and a Winchester held in his right hand. He looked like he was coming from the wilderness country that divided the Arizona Territory from California, and Weaver figured his horse must have died somewhere along the trail; but he hadn't asked after the man looked at him. He had walked straight up to the way station and demanded tickets through to Galveston. Weaver had explained that the Southern Pacific hadn't got around to running a spur line down to the coast yet, so they'd compromised on a through billet to Houston.

The man had given his name as Matthew Gunn.

Now he dumped the saddle by the ticket window and walked off towards the straggle of buildings that made up Brandon's Hole.

The place – it couldn't be called a town – was built around the seepage well discovered by Carl Brandon when he was prospecting for gold. The water had paid off better than a mine and for the price of hard work, a busted leg, and three bullet wounds administered by drovers who objected to paying for water, Brandon had wound up a rich man. When the Southern Pacific brought the tracks through the territory, old Carl had sold out, packed up and gone to booze himself to death in New Orleans. The railroad had built a water tank, a timber-and-tar depot hut, and a hash house. An optimistic Texan had erected a one-storey saloon with beds in back, and since the country quieted down some, other traders had moved in. Brandon's Hole grew to boast a rooming house – with whores as part of the service – a couple of stores and a handful of permanent inhabitants. They kidded themselves that one day they'd have a real town with a marshal and a mayor, maybe even a doctor. But that was a long way off.

The man called Gunn spat dust from a dry mouth and made for the saloon.

He pushed through the flap of hide making shift for a door and walked up to the bar. It was three planks nailed together with cross-beams and set on two barrels. A roughly lettered sign advertised beer, tequila and whisky, with water fetching the same price as hard liquor. He ordered beer and a bottle, carrying the mug of frothy amber liquid over to a corner table, then going back for the whisky. He used his left hand: the right still held the carbine.

The interior of the saloon was dark, the adobe walls and narrow windows holding out the heat so that it stayed cool inside. At the far end of the room, three cowhands tippled whisky over a desultory poker game.

One looked up at the stranger.

'You wanta sit in? We could use some fresh blood.'

'No thanks.' Gunn's voice was deep, his accent curiously guttural, as though English was not his native tongue.

The cowboys caught the inflection and glanced at one another, wondering. The man who had spoken grinned and stood up. He sauntered over to the stove built into one corner of the room, pouring coffee. Then he ambled across to the far end and stood watching the blond man.

Gunn had removed his stetson, letting the mane of pale hair tumble around his face. He was sipping beer, his eyes fixed on the doorway. The cowboy watched him in silence, then shifted around to block the view.

'What kinda accent's that?'

His own was a nasal Texas twang.

Gunn looked up, his eyes steady. 'Why?'

'Waal,' the cowboy looked across at his friends, weighing up their chances of enlivening a boring afternoon, 'it sounded kinda funny to me.'

'So laugh.' Gunn poured whisky and swallowed a shot.

'You ain't exactly conversational, are you?' The cowboy moved closer to the table, peering hard at the seated man. 'You look kinda odd, come to think of it. Them injun boots, an' all.'

'Mister,' said Matthew Gunn softly, guessing what was coming, 'why don't you go sit down? Play poker an' leave me be.'

'You know?' The cowboy pushed his point. 'You sound kinda like an 'injun. You a breed, or sumthin'?'

Gunn took a deep breath and let it out slowly. The whole scene was like an old memory: he had played it through before and he knew how it would end. *Hell,* he thought, *I gave the man a chance. I asked him to go away, so now it's up to him.*

'Yeah,' he said evenly, 'I am. My mother was Chiricahua Apache. My paw was white.'

'Hey, boy!' The Texan's voice was louder, pitched to carry over to his friends. 'You ain't got no right to be in here. This's a white man's saloon.'

'There's no sign says that.' Gunn kept his voice steady.

'I'm tellin' you,' grinned the cowboy. It wasn't a pleasant grin. 'No injuns.'

He turned away, reaching for the chalk stick resting on the bar. The owner was ostentatiously polishing clean glasses, doing his best to rub the bottoms away. The Texan motioned for his buddies to join him and headed back to Gunn's table. He set his mug down and reached over with the chalk. Laboriously, he printed out a message on the scrubbed wood: *No injuns. Not welcum.*

Gunn kept his hands on the table, waiting for the man to finish. The cowboy stood upright, reaching for the coffee mug.

Gunn reached it first. He came to his feet with the tin cup in his left hand, lifting up fast. The steaming coffee splashed into the Texan's face and he yelled as the hot liquid hit his eyes, staining his shirt front.

'Now you got grounds to complain,' snarled Gunn.

He tipped the table as he said it, throwing the heavy wood forwards so that it crashed against the man's legs, pitching him over backwards. He hit the plank floor with a thud, screaming as the edge of the table landed across his ankles. Gunn stepped around the fallen table as the other two halted halfway down the bar.

'Sweet Jesus!' The first cowpoke doubled over, clutching at his legs. 'My fuckin' legs are broke.'

'You want a fight? Or you gone far enough?'

Gunn's voice was calm, tinged with a mixture of harsh Apache and Scottish burr.

'You done crippled Jed,' gasped one cowboy.

'He asked for it,' said Gunn.

'Motherin' injun!' The speaker was wiry, mean-looking. And fast. His pistol was lifting as he spoke.

Gunn was faster. The Colt came up out of the holster with the speed of long practice and natural talent. His thumb hauled the hammer back as the heavy revolver lined on the man's stomach, the index finger holding the trigger down so that the gun went off as the muzzle aligned with the Texan's rib-cage.

The cowboy grunted and seemed to jump back, away from the crimson stain that flowered suddenly over the front of his shirt. Abruptly, he dropped his own gun and sat down as though his legs had folded under him. He clenched both hands over his belly, doubling forwards until his head touched the floor. He moaned, and the planks between his feet became red.

Gunn powered across the room. He dropped his left hand onto the bar, pivoting as he swung forwards and up. Both feet hit the second Texan in the chest, spinning him back as he fumbled with the .44 Remington cross-hung from his waist. Gunn landed on his feet, his right arm swinging in a round-house blow that smashed the barrel of the Colt against the side of the cowboy's jaw. The man's head snapped sideways and a fragment of tooth spat from between his lips. Gunn brought the Colt back in a short, vicious arc that layed the barrel hard on the Texan's neck. It hit where the neck joins the shoulder, where the heavy nerve clusters gather to run up into the brain. The Texan opened his mouth and dropped another tooth. His eyes glazed over and he crumpled sideways onto the floor.

Gunn spun around, levelling the Colt on Jed.

The original troublemaker was crouched beside the overturned table, holding his right leg with both hands, his eyes wide and frightened.

'No!' His voice held a high, screeching note of naked fear. 'I ain't in it!' He looked at his fallen friends and turned wide open eyes back to Gunn. 'Jeeze! I never seen nuthin' like it. I'm sorry, mister. I never thought...'

Gunn ended the sentence with the butt of the Colt. Flipping the gun so that the handle stuck out from his fist, he slammed it into Jed's mouth. The cowboy flopped back against the table, his eyes looking at nothing as blood trickled from his lips lacerated by shattered teeth.

The barkeep was still polishing glasses, and the shot cowboy was still coughing blood over his boots. Around the door, a tight knot of faces gazed inwards, enjoying the first excitement Brandon's Hole had seen in months. Gunn looked towards them, and the watchers drew back. He smiled tightly, dropping the Colt back into the holster. Then he picked up his Winchester and the whisky bottle, and made for the door.

'If someone patches him fast enough,' he gestured at the wounded Texan, 'he might live. When they come around, tell them that Indians are people, too.'

The bartender nodded dumbly, and watched Gunn walk out of the place.

Someone in the crowd began to mutter something about Indians, but when he caught the eye of the blond man with the carbine he closed his mouth. And kept it that way until the breed was out of earshot. After that, the citizens of Brandon's Hole crowded into the saloon and the barkeep set to serving drinks while he recounted the full story of the shooting. It was the best day's business he'd had in a long time, and while he made money the shot Texan died.

As he bled his life away, the man who had killed him was

sprawled in the shade of the depot hut's overhanging porch, sipping whisky and thinking.

It had taken him a little over three months to reach Brandon's Hole and he was angry with himself for attempting the journey from San Francisco on horseback. It had been a decision prompted by impatience and the absence of an immediate sea passage. The men he hunted had left on a coast-hugging vessel and he had ridden south and east in a fury of revenge. Now, with California and four dead horses behind him, he hoped to pick up the trail in Texas.

It was, he had to admit, a pretty long shot, but it was the best he had. So he relaxed in the shade, waiting for the train to pull in.

He grinned, thinking of the cowhands back in the saloon. Whites were strangely intolerant, not like his mother's people.

Matthew Gunn was the son of the Apache woman, Rainbow Hair, and a Santa Fe trader called Kieron Gunn. He had been raised amongst the Chiricahuas in the lonely stronghold of the Sierra Mogollon, a halfbreed youngster with the traits of both his parents' races. Tough as any Apache, he had a white education behind him, imparted by his dead father. The thought thinned his lips in anger. His parents – his whole rancheria – had been wiped out by scalp hunters. Now he hunted the last of the killers: two men. The others were dead* and Matthew Gunn, who was called Azul by his mother's people, intended to complete his revenge.

The two men were called Nolan and Jude Christie.

He slumped with the total relaxation only an Indian seemed capable of achieving, listening to the flies that buzzed lazily around his face. Brandon's Hole had lapsed back into its customary indolence, with no-one ready to take up the Texan's cause and the next big event the mid-afternoon stop of the Southern Pacific's Texas-bound train.

Gunn – Azul – dozed in the heated shade.

*See: Breed - The Lonely Hunt and The Silent Kill

A shrieking sound like some great animal in pain brought him to his feet in a single clean movement. The howling echoed again, shrill and lonely, in the empty land, and he saw a thin plume of rising smoke that spouted up before dispersing in the higher air. Slowly at first, then faster as she came around the curve of track leading into Brandon's Hole, the train grew larger. The outline of a high-stacked 4-4-0 locomotive shaped itself through the heat haze, the sun reflecting bright off the warning lamps set above the dusty vee of the cowcatcher. The whistle shrilled again, and steam erupted from around the massive drive wheels as the big loco began to brake.

Gunn saw two carriages behind the engine, then a bleached-wood freight wagon and the stubby bulk of the brake-car. The entire rig squealed and gusted steam as the wheels locked and she slid to a precise stop alongside the low platform. A uniformed porter swung a folding ladder down from the forward carriage, and jumped onto the platform as Ben Weaver swung the elongated trunk of the water hose over to the engineer.

Gunn let the porter take his saddle and climbed on board. The carriage was half empty, the passengers occupying the hard, wood seats glancing incuriously at the new traveller. He found an empty bench and showed the conductor the length of perforated tickets as the porter stowed the saddle beneath the seat. Then he stretched his legs out and went back to sleep.

The engineer filled the tank, sounded the whistle one last time, and shoved the locomotive into gear. She hauled out, gathering speed, heading along the Gila River towards Tucson, El Paso and San Antonio.

Soon Brandon's Hole was lost in the haze, one more forgotten stop-over on the long journey East.

As the loco pulled out, Nolan and Christie were riding slowly along the upper fork of the Colorado. They carried Winchesters across their saddles and their eyes scanned the surrounding country with unceasing vigilance. Between them, and slightly to the rear, came a small, canvas-topped wagon drawn by a team of four big horses. The driver was a grizzled oldster, more adept at handling a team than in making conversation with the woman seated beside him. She looked, anyway, too fatigued by the heat to want to talk. She was a handsome-looking woman in her early thirties, not yet old enough to have lost all her youthful looks, but sufficiently experienced to know her way around.

Her name was Eleanor Dalton, and she was married to the owner of the Flying D spread on the headwaters of the Colorado.

She had spent the last three months with her family in St. Louis, then taken a river boat down the Mississippi to New Orleans, a stage west to Houston, and then hired a wagon and driver to cover the last part of her journey back to the ranch.

The Flying D was situated on the south-eastern edge of the Llano Estacado, a growing venture built with blood, sweat and raw endurance. Nathaniel Dalton had staked his claim right after the Civil War, when the land was open for the taking and the newly united states crying out for beef. With two cowhands and a crippled cook, he had lived under canvas until they got around to building a soddy. Two years and three trail drives later, he got to building a wood and stone ranch house. During those twenty four months he fought off Kiowa and Comanche, rustlers and drought, wolves and freezing winters. He sank wells and built corrals, and slowly the spread grew. With better than three thousand cows foraging his domain, Nathaniel decided his collateral was good enough to start thinking about his old age. He decided to get married. Leaving the ranch in the care of his foreman, he rode down to San Antonio, to the rail depot. He ended up in St. Louis, staying at the Mansion House Hotel trying hard to learn the rules of Eastern society. At a ball, he met Miss Eleanor Denton, eldest daughter of a minor family. One month, seven balls, five picnics and three – to Nathaniel, excruciatingly boring – visits to the opera later, they were married. He took his bride back with him to Texas.

At first, Eleanor was entranced with the rugged land and her equally rugged husband. The years and the country had blunted the edges of the romance, and something solid, as durable as the age-worn mesas of the surrounding country, had grown between them. Now Eleanor was Mizz Dalton, the boss's wife, and knew near as much about the running of the Flying D as Nathaniel himself.

Her visit to St. Louis was the first in three years. And it sounded like she had picked the worst possible time to make it.

From New Orleans westwards, she had heard increasingly alarming rumours of Indian trouble. Houston and San Antonio were alive with gossip of Comanche raids, slaughtered cattle and wrecked stage coaches. A Ranger captain had warned her against travelling unescorted, confirming reports of at least three outlying homesteads massacred by Indians. The tribes were getting hold of guns, too often Spencer, Henry or Winchester repeaters, but the Comancheros stayed elusive – and active. She had begun to look for reliable men willing to hire on as outriders.

She had found them one hot afternoon outside her hotel.

She had just eaten luncheon – in some ways she still adhered to the niceties of St. Louis society – and planned to take a walk, when a drunk had presented himself as a dependable escort. She was doing her best to fob the man off when he turned nasty. His abuse was approaching an alarmingly imaginative climax when a voice that was simultaneously quiet and harsh stopped him in mid-sentence. He turned around, glaring at the speaker: a tall man in black, with cold, green eyes that stared with open contempt.

'Fuck off.' The drunk was a big man and his voice was loud.

The man in black said nothing. Instead, he kicked the drunk very hard in the groin. The drunk shrilled like a stuck pig and started to double up, but his progress was abruptly arrested by the other man's knee. It rammed into the drunk's face, and as he toppled sideways, the dark man hit him again, behind the left ear.

The drunk collapsed into the street and the green-eyed man smiled.

'Ma'am,' he murmured, 'I trust you're alright?'

'Thank you, yes,' Eleanor had replied, thinking fast. 'I wonder if I might talk with you.'

As they went back inside the Imperial Hotel, she noted the way he wore his gun, the contained energy of his movements. Most of all she noted his eyes.

An hour later, Nolan – it was the only name he offered – had agreed to escort Mrs. Dalton back to her home.

A day later, they became lovers. It was a calculated move on both their parts, prompted by boredom and a tacit recognition of like minds. Eleanor Dalton had enjoyed three lovers since her wedding. One was a young cowboy who spoiled a tidy arrangement by falling off his horse in the middle of a stampede; the second was a distant cousin she met on an earlier trip to St. Louis; the third, a gambler on a river boat. Nolan, the fourth, was the most exciting. He was good in bed, but it was the barely-hidden violence that emanated from him like a tangible aura that sent the shivers through Eleanor's fulsome body. There was something about the man that spoke of danger, of ruthlessness; Eleanor enjoyed it.

On Nolan's part it was a mixture of lust and a feeling that the woman might prove useful. She had money, a ranch, and a husband she obviously didn't care too much about. Given the right opportunities, she might just provide him with a new base from which to hunt scalps. So he agreed to take her home, accompanied by Jude Christie.

Now they were deep into Comanche territory, with open country all around and God knew how many Indians ready to lift their hair.

Sign aplenty had shown along the way, although no attack had come. Yet. They had seen cattle rotting, bellies ripped open by Comanche lances and left to die. Two days back, they had spotted a burned-out wagon. The three corpses they found had been smelly and ugly to look at. No-one had suggested burying them.

A mood of foreboding hung over the Staked Plains like the nerve-tingling silence that precedes a bad storm. It was the hottest summer Nolan could remember, and there seemed to be more vultures patrolling the sky than was normal. For three days now he and Christie had ridden with their carbines across their saddles, ready for instant use. They rode mostly in silence, too intent on watching and listening to risk slackening their vigilance in conversation. It was beginning to tell on Christie's nerves, and Nolan was glad the ranch lay only two more days' travelling away.

Samuel Graves shared Nolan's sense of impending danger, had done so since sighting the mirage. He told himself it was ridiculous, but it made no difference, he was unable to shake the feeling.

Jaime Sanchez tried to laugh it off, but that just made Graves angry: his partner sat safe in Mexico buying the guns, it was Graves who had to cross the border and deal with Iron Knife.

Their rendezvous point was a tiny town called Quintana, a half day's ride south from the Rio Grande. An unwritten agreement – and discreet bribes – kept the Federales off the Comancheros' backs, and the town was accepted as a centre of free enterprise. Now Graves and Sanchez were planning the negro's return trip to the Staked Plains.

Sanchez had spent the past month collecting rifles. He had invested a fair proportion of their bankroll in Mexico and the United States, buying up repeating rifles wherever he could find them. In a straw-thatched barn on the outskirts of Quintana there were nearly two hundred assorted weapons and thirty crates of ammunition. It was the biggest investment they had ever made, and it promised the greatest reward. But Graves had doubts about the advisability of shipping everything at once. Sanchez was trying to talk his partner into it.

'*Mirar,*' he argued, 'we stand to make one big killing, no? Iron Knife has the gold, we have the guns. One trip, Samuel, that's all. Just one. Then we take things easy.'

'Yeah.' Graves swallowed tequila. 'It's easy for you, ain't it? You sit back safe. It's me that goes out to meet him.'

'But Samuel,' Sanchez wheedled, 'Iron Knife trusts you. You know the Comanches look on your kind as brothers. I'm just another white man to them, little different than the *americanos*. The colour of your skin is a passport.'

Graves couldn't refute the argument. It was a fact that the Indians considered negros to be more or less the same as the red men. It was why he was so successful; that and Sanchez' genius for locating weapons. But he still couldn't shake the uneasy feeling. The Comanches were preparing for something, something big, and he didn't want to be around when it broke.

But money was money, and profit was the name of the game. Samuel Graves intended to die a rich man: he just hoped he could stay alive long enough to enjoy his wealth.

'Alright, Jaime,' he muttered reluctantly. 'I'll do it. But after, we take things easy for a spell.'

'*Bueno!*' Sanchez slapped the spreading weight of his belly in appreciation. 'When will you leave?'

'Tomorrow,' answered Graves, 'at sun-up.'

He rose, calling for old Paco. He issued instructions, ignoring the Mexican's doubtful look: it reminded him too much of his own misgivings.

Matthew Gunn tossed his saddle down to the platform and climbed off the train. He stood for a moment, watching the bustle of the Houston & Texas Central station. Cities still made him feel uncomfortable and he hoped he could pick up Nolan's trail fast, and move on out to the open spaces.

A porter approached him, asking if he had any baggage. Gunn shook his head, picking up the saddle. The man grunted, pointing at it.

'You got yore saddle, mister. Don't get hoarse answering.'

CHAPTER THREE

Matthew Gunn was wanted in Texas. Hunting the killers of his parents, he had crossed a Texas Ranger and been forced into a gunfight. The Rangers had posted a $200 reward when the man died, and – Gunn knew – they had long memories. Houston, a Ranger stronghold, was not the healthiest place he could be. But the implacable desire for revenge that had driven him south from New Mexico across the border, and back into Texas, on through Arizona and Nevada to California and, now, back full circle to Texas, brooked no denying. He wanted Nolan and Christie, and he had come too far to turn back.

Caution prompted him to locate a cheap rooming house in a relatively quiet section of the city. No questions were asked and for the first time in months he enjoyed the luxury of a hot bath and a soft bed. Before sleeping, however, he decided to check the hotels. Like the jibes about his accent, the routine was familiar and irksome. He walked from place to place, asking bored desk clerks if they had seen two men, one dark, one fair. Mostly, the clerks were too bored to bother much about remembering and the few who tried couldn't recall anyone fitting the descriptions.

Until he reached the Imperial.

It was an imposing building, all of three storeys tall with a false frontage that rose still higher. A liveried doorman curled his lip as Gunn walked in, and the clerk made a fuss of the register when he approached the desk. The vestibule was lit bright by ornate lamps, the kerosene flames illuminating the gleaming brasswork and plush velvet chairs. Gilt framed mirrors reflected the entire room and frock-coated men looked disapprovingly at his travel-stained clothes. The women with them, most wearing full-length evening gowns, looked with considerably more interest at his lean body and roughly-handsome face.

Finally, when he let the dollar in his fist clink onto the desk, the clerk gave up his perusal of the register and came over.

'Yes?' There was a noticeable pause before he added, 'Sir.'

Gunn described his quarry and the clerk's eyes flickered with quickly-veiled interest. He began to mumble something about not recalling the gentlemen when a second coin jogged his memory.

'No, wait. I believe I do have a notion.'

A third coin confirmed it and *sir* became part of his vocabulary again.

'Why yes, sir.' He screwed his small eyes into wrinkled pouches with the effort. 'That would be Mrs. Dalton's, umm, *friend.* A tall man. Dark. Green eyes. Fond of black. Mrs. Dalton *entertained* him frequently.' He winked lewdly, the silver dollars establishing friendship. 'I never caught his name, but he was often to be seen with another gentleman. A fair-haired man with a Southern accent. They were both . . .'

'Where'd they go?' Gunn's question stopped the clerk in mid-flow.

'I really couldn't say.' Then the clerk saw the impatience burning in Gunn's eyes and revised his opinion. 'Well, wait. I do believe that Mrs. Dalton hired them both to escort her home. The Flying D ranch,' he added hurriedly, 'on the Staked Plains, near the north fork of the Colorado.'

'When?' Gunn's voice was harsh, urgent.

'Two weeks ago. They'll be travelling slow. They had a wagon.'

The last words were shouted at Gunn's back. He was already moving fast from the hotel, pushing through the guests gathering around the door, ignoring the angry retorts of the men he elbowed aside. They spluttered and complained, but when they saw his face they fell back and let him pass unhindered.

It was full dark by the time he got back to the rooming house, and wide-spaced street lights were burning along the back alleys. The owner was in the kitchen, his feet up on a pot-bellied stove as he pored laboriously over the large type of a penny-dreadful claiming to be the authentic story of the gallant James gang. It was written by someone called James Harknett and Gunn doubted the man had been farther west than Philadelphia. It must have been interesting reading, because the owner, a balding man called Harvey, didn't look up when Gunn entered.

'I need a horse.'

His tone was urgent enough to pull Harvey's eyes away from his book.

'Stable's two blocks down, one across.' Harvey turned back to the daring exploits of Jesse and Frank. 'Most likely shut down by now, though.'

Gunn took a chance on that and left the rooming house in a hurry. Harvey was right: the stable was closed, a note pinned to the door announcing that the proprietor could be located in the Alamo saloon. Gunn found him drinking whisky.

'I need a horse.'

'I need a drink. Come back at sun-up.'

'Now.'

'Mister,' the stableman was a white-maned oldster with most of his teeth missing, 'the stable's closed an' the horses bedded down. I figger to follow 'em before long, so whyn't you buy yoreself a drink an' take it easy. I'll attend to you in the mornin'.'

Gunn's hand fell on his shoulder, closed around a fold of grubby linen, and the ostler felt himself lifted from his chair. He gagged, spitting whisky over the table, and his feet tried to find the floor.

'Now,' said Gunn.

A younger man, sitting across from the oldster made to rise. Gunn glanced at him.

'I wouldn't,' he shook his head slightly, 'not if you want to stay healthy.'

The man sat down again.

Gunn frog-marched the stablehand from the saloon, ignoring his complaints as he pushed the old man before him along the sidewalk. They reached the stable and pushed inside. The oldster lit a match, fumbling for a lantern. When the wick caught, he gestured irritably at the horses.

'Take yore pick. The bay an' the black are put up fer the night. The chestnut ain't fer sale an' the skewbald's lame. 'Part from that you kin have whichever takes yore fancy.'

Gunn took the lantern and inspected the animals. Five of them were pack horses and useless for his purpose, two more looked stringy, weak, but the eighth seemed a possible mount. It was a big roan gelding that looked to be a cross between a quarter-horse and a mustang. When he slid into the stall it rolled its eyes and snickered nervously, showing yellow teeth as it blew air through wide-spread nostrils. Gunn murmured softly in lilting Spanish, reaching out to stroke the animal's muzzle. After a while it calmed down and he knelt to inspect its legs. They were smooth-muscled with a powerful look to them, matching the deep chest and lean, glossy flanks. It looked like a pony with speed and staying power, the kind of animal that could take punishment and come back for more.

He nodded appreciatively and opened the stall.

'I'll give you one thing,' remarked the stableman grudgingly. 'You got better taste in horseflesh than you got manners. Ole Red there's one o' the best animals I seen in a long time.'

'How much?' Gunn asked.

'Sixty dollars,' grunted the oldster.

'Go to hell. I'll pay thirty.'

'Fifty, on account you spoiled my drinkin'.'

'Thirty-five.'

'Make it forty-five an' I'll throw in a bridle.'

'Make it forty an' I'll pay you.'

'Done.'

The old man spat tobacco juice into the straw. He walked down to the end of the barn where the tack hung in an empty stall. Gunn followed him.

'No,' he said when the man offered him a worn bridle. 'That one.'

He pointed to a newer set of tackle, the leather polished and the bit and buckles showing no signs of rust.

'Shit,' grumbled the oldster, 'I thought I was the horsetrader round here.'

Gunn smiled and counted greenbacks into a calloused hand. Then he fixed the tack around the horse's head and swung astride. The stableman noticed that he mounted from the right, Indian fashion, and scratched his scalp speculatively.

'You got injun blood, mister?'

'Yeah,' replied Gunn, tensing for a new argument, 'you got objections?'

'Hell, no.' More tobacco hit the floor. 'Far as I'm concerned any injun's a good injun if he's got money.'

Gunn chuckled and heeled the pony forward. He rode it back to the rooming house and saddled up. Harvey demanded a full night's money for the room and agreed to sell five dollars' worth of provisions. Gunn figured that would be enough to see him through to the Flying D. He didn't want to stop along the way to hunt and he could pick up more food at the ranch. After he had killed Nolan and Christie.

He turned the pony's head north and west, and quit Houston at a fast canter.

Nolan lay back and looked at the stars. They were big and bright, just like the song said; too damn' bright. The moon was three-quarters full, a huge, pale yellow disc that looked close enough to touch and lit the badlands near as bright as day. A little bit longer and it would be full: a Comanche moon, the kind the Indians believed was bright enough to guide the dead to the spirit world, even if it was night when they died.

He listened for a moment, then turned to the woman beside him.

Eleanor Dalton stretched naked on a spread blanket, the moonlight outlining the sensuous contours of her body. The sight of her stirred his loins and he reached across, stroking her breasts.

She rolled sideways, pulling him to her, between her parted legs. Nolan grinned and thrust against her, his right arm shifting over to check the Colt set carefully on the blanket. For a little while he forgot about the danger.

'This will be the last time.' Her voice was a husky whisper in his ear. 'We'll reach home tomorrow.'

'It ain't dawn yet,' muttered Nolan, 'so it ain't the last time.'

The woman ignored his boast. 'What will you do when we get to the Flying D?'

'Why, ma'am,' chuckled Nolan, 'I'll deliver you back to yore lovin' husband an' collect his money for doin' my duty by his wife.'

'Oh damn it,' murmured Eleanor, 'I wish it was different. I wish you didn't have to ride on.'

Nolan stared out across the empty desert. In the moonlight his green eyes appeared almost luminous.

'Maybe,' he muttered, too low for her to hear, 'I won't.'

They slept for a spell, then woke and made love again. Afterwards, Nolan climbed to his feet, pulling on his pants. A vague plan was beginning to form in his mind, though it would take a close look at the Flying D and its owner before anything crystallised. Eleanor Dalton was halfway in love with him, he could sense that even though she had never said it, and he had gone out of his way to encourage her. Sneaking off nights to tumble on a dusty blanket was part of it: in normal circumstances, he was sure, she would have been far too discreet to throw herself so openly into an affair. That she had was both pleasant and useful; he knew she was fully capable of dropping him once they reached the spread, but he doubted she could forget him too easily.

He grinned and buckled his gunbelt around his waist.

The sky was paling into dawn and birds were beginning to sing. The plains smelled fresh, and he could hear the tiny desert animals skittering into hiding as the sun came up. Over by the wagon the driver, Jack Street, was blowing the fire to new life under the coffee pot and Jude Christie was grumbling reluctantly out of his bedroll.

Nolan shook the woman awake and went to find coffee while she dressed. Christie leered at him from across the fire and started to say something. The look on Nolan's face shut him up. Fast. Nolan had that effect on people. Eleanor joined them, ignoring Christie's grin and Street's poker-faced disapproval. She climbed into the wagon, re-appearing with her hair combed and a crisp, new dress. A poke bonnet sat demurely on her blonde hair and she looked like the self-satisfied wife of a wealthy rancher.

'Why, Mizz Dalton,' grinned Christie, lifting his hat, 'you look real fine, dressed up an' all to meet yore husband.'

Her eyes blazed, but it was Nolan's voice that wiped the grin from his partner's face.

'Jude,' he said quietly, 'you got a fat mouth. Best close it afore I shove somethin' through it.'

Jack Street sniggered and began to hand out plates. They ate breakfast in silence and rode out the same way, Nolan and Christie moving out ahead of the wagon, anxious to reach the Flying D.

They were about ten miles away from the ranch buildings, well into Dalton land, when the Comanches showed. A line of Indians appeared out of nowhere ahead and to the side of their path. The leader raised a war lance and a high-pitched, yammering shriek split the early morning air. Then the Indians charged.

CHAPTER FOUR

Samuel Graves called an early halt when the mesa came in sight. It was the same eroded tumble of sandy stone the Comancheros had used on their earlier journey, now Graves planned to use it again – to buy him a little insurance.

He turned his horse, watching the pack train go by. Paco handled a four-horse team hauling a flat-bed wagon with canvas concealing the crated rifles. A younger Mexican, Enrico, rode shotgun. The halfbreed, John Bear, and a Mexican called Hernando occupied the second wagon, loaded high with ammunition. Six outriders flanked the wagons, hard-eyed pistoleros selected personally by Graves for their skill with weapons and their indifference to death.

Graves wiped sweat from his jaw and brought his mount up alongside Paco's wagon.

'Get 'em in close to the rock, *amigo*. Then make camp.'

'*Si, jefe,*' Paco nodded, urging the team forwards.

He took the rig in amongst the fallen boulders and pushed the brake down. John Bear and Hernando followed, bringing the ammunition wagon up alongside the other. The pistoleros dismounted and two of them, without waiting for orders, climbed the mesa and crouched down, watching. Graves liked that: it was one of the reasons he had picked these men. They were professionals and on this trip he felt the need of reliable guns.

The halfbreeds set to collecting buffalo chips and John Bear got a fire going as Paco broke out food and coffee. It was late afternoon and Graves wanted twilight before he set to work.

By the time they had eaten the day was losing its brightness. The sun threw long shadows across the flat terrain and the desert grew curiously still, the quality of the light altered from the eye-watering glare of day to the deceptively luminous tranquility that comes before the sudden arrival of full darkness. It was still light enough to see, but not for far; it was time.

Graves hauled a spade from the side of one wagon and tossed it to Enrico.

'Alright.' He dug a heel into the sand as he spoke. 'Let's get to diggin'.'

'*Que es?*' Paco was curious. 'Why do we dig?'

Graves smiled, pleased with himself.

'We're carryin' near on two hundred repeaters, right? An' enough ammunition to fight Bull Run over again. We deliver that lot to Iron Knife in one package an' he's got more guns than he's ever seen before. It might just turn his evil head an' set him thinkin' he don't need us anymore.'

Paco nodded slowly, his eyes thoughtful.

'So,' continued Graves, 'I figger to bury 'bout half the load here. We take the rest on to ole Knife an' when we're sure of his honourable intentions we tell him where to find the remainder. He ain't gonna be sure we told him the truth, so he has to keep us alive.'

'*Muy bueno,*' grinned Paco approvingly, '*seguro.*'

'Yeah,' said Graves. 'Insurance. I'm a prudential kinda o' guy.'

They took it in turns to dig, excavating a pit deep enough to take half the rifles and five crates of shells. It was dark by the time they finished and Graves walked two of the horses back and forth over the disturbed sand. When he was satisfied the weapons were completely hidden they settled down for the night.

Out on the desert, a coyote looked up at the filling moon, raised its lean, grey head and howled. The lonely sound seemed to go on for ever and Paco shifted uneasily in his bedroll, a sudden shiver tingling down the length of his spine.

'*Santa Maria,*' he muttered, 'someone just walked on my grave.'

They moved out at sun-up, making better time with the lightened wagons, and reached the meeting place close on noon. There was no sign of Iron Knife and his warriors. The Pecos lay behind them, and somewhere to the west was the Colorado. Graves felt edgy. Fort Stockton was a hundred-odd miles to the south and he was worried about long-range cavalry patrols. With the kind of trouble the territory had seen during the past months, it was likely the Army would put out riders to check the isolated ranches of the Llano Estacado; equally, the Texas Rangers could be scouting the country. Their feud with the Comanches was long-standing and bloody, and what little time they had for Comancheros was limited to the minutes it takes to drop a hanging rope over a handy tree.

Shaded by the wagons, the renegades waited.

They waited all through the long afternoon and on into the night. In the morning Graves decided to take a chance. He had sent scouts out and they reported back without sighting anyone in the big emptiness. He built a signal fire. It was made of buffalo chips and a dampened blanket, murky smoke lifting up in a straight line into the sky.

After a while the Comanches came.

Paco saw them first, and nudged Graves to instant wakefulness. The negro came out from under the wagon, shading his eyes with one upraised hand, peering through the heat haze that distorted the shapes of the riders.

The horsemen approached in single file, walking their ponies casually towards the waiting Comancheros. There were only five of them, and Graves couldn't spot Iron Knife amongst them. Individual warriors were hard to recognise beneath the paint covering their bodies. Broad bands of black, red or white decorated arms and legs, torsos not covered by the protective quill chest bibs were painted with medicine symbols, and streaks of colour camouflaged the contours of broad faces. The mustangs were painted, too, and both men and animals wore feathers and small, brightly-coloured medicine pouches.

They carried no firearms, but each warrior bore a lance and shield, and most had bows slung behind them on the ponies' withers.

They approached with a total disregard of the Comancheros' guns, or the fact that they were outnumbered.

'War paint,' murmured Paco, close by Graves' left.

'Yeah,' replied the black man, 'I guess whatever it is they're plannin' is about to break.'

He plastered a friendly smile across his mouth and lifted both hands, palms outwards, waiting for the Indians to reach him.

They came level with the wagons and fanned out, one warrior moving forward from the centre of the semi-circle.

'I am Little Buffalo.' His English was surprisingly good. 'Iron Knife send me. You come, bring wagons to camp.'

'Where's Iron Knife?' Graves was wary.

'In camp.'

'Why didn't he come? He knew we was meetin' here.' Graves held his ground.

'Iron Knife purifies himself,' answered Little Buffalo. 'He seeks his dream.'

Graves grunted. The set-up began to worry him.

'What about the gold?'

'Bring guns to camp. Gold there.'

'Why not here?' The negro didn't like the idea of entering a village full of hostiles.

'Iron Knife say *come.*' Little Buffalo was tired of arguing. 'You want gold, you come.'

He backed his mustang away from Graves, heeling the animal round so that its tail faced the Comanchero. Without another word he rode away, followed by the others.

'Hell,' Graves shrugged, 'I guess we better follow 'em.'

He climbed onto his horse, motioning for his men to mount up, and set out after the Indians.

Towards dusk they reached the Comanche village. It was situated in a shallow depression, a half-mile saucer scooped from the centre of the Staked Plains with a small spring bubbling out of the desert. It was the biggest camp the Comancheros had ever seen, and it set Graves' nerves violently on edge. Children and women clustered round as they came in, calling out in the guttural, clicking tongue of the horse tribes. Graves got the feeling that a wrong move, however minimal, would engulf them in a mob of shrieking, blood-hungry squaws. He had heard what they did to captives.

Keeping his eyes fixed firmly on Little Buffalo's painted back, he followed the Indian to the centre of the camp.

Adhering to custom, the Comancheros stayed in their saddles until they were invited to dismount. Warriors led their horses off to a picket line, and two Indians guided the wagons to an open space between two rings of hide wigwams.

'Wait.' Little Buffalo gestured at a big lodge, indicating they should enter. 'Iron Knife will come.'

He walked away, his gait a bow-legged, rolling movement typical of men who live on horseback. The Comancheros went into the lodge: there was nothing else to do.

'How many you reckon?' Graves asked Paco.

'Six, maybe seven hundred,' replied the old Mexican. 'I never saw a bigger camp.'

'Nor so much paint,' added Enrico.

'*Si,*' murmured Paco. 'I think our friends are planning to start a war.'

Gunn – Azul – knew that a big and bloody storm was about to break over the Staked Plains. For anyone with eyes trained to spot the signs of trouble, the desert read like a book.

Two days out of Houston he had found the marks of cattle run off the range. The unshod Indian ponies left hoofprints that spelled out *Comanche* in capital letters. The slaughtered cows he found the next day meant it was both a food-gathering and a vengeance raid. The homestead confirmed it. It was a three-room soddy, built up against a rock outcrop so the 'steaders were protected from the rear. The Comanches had overcome that problem by the simple expedient of driving the rancher's own beeves up the gradient and over the edge. The roof of the soddy was stove in, dead cows littered the stained floor. The rancher hung from one wall, held upright by the nails driven through his hands. His belly was a fly-infested hole with arrows sticking out from amongst the spilled entrails.

His eyes still retained the look of horror that had filled them as he died staring at his wife.

The woman sprawled on the sand fronting the shack, a column of busy ants scurrying around her naked scalp. Dried blood caked her inner thighs and stomach and her legs twisted around at ugly angles. Gunn wondered if the Comanches had broken them before they raped her.

Six feet away, a hairless boy of about fourteen clutched a broken shotgun. Spinal bone showed where a hatchet had broken his back, and the stump of his left wrist indicated ritual mutilation. The severed hand was stuck in his mother's mouth.

Gunn spat and rode away: the corpses stank.

He moved cautiously, noting the tracks criss-crossing the badlands. Some belonged to war bands, others to tribal groups. All moved towards a central point somewhere to his north. The Comanches were gathering in force, like red storm clouds joining to rain chaos over the land. And it looked as though the Flying D would be close to the storm's centre. He grinned savagely: the Comanches were traditional enemies of the Apache, he would enjoy killing them.

On the sixth day he spotted wagon tracks heading in the same direction as the Indians. Two teams of four horses each had pulled a heavy load northwards not long ago. About six men had escorted the wagons, and they had camped beside a low mesa.

Something about the camp worried him, and he stayed longer than he had intended.

Then he realised what it was: the ground showed signs of around a dozen horses picketed to one side of a buffalo chip fire, but the area to the other side showed almost as many hoofprints, as though someone had walked the animals back and forth over the soil. He drew his Bowie knife and scraped at the sandy dirt. The blade went in easily and struck something solid. A few minutes later he knew it was a wooden crate: the hoofprints were intended to hide a cache.

Curious, he began to uncover the crate. Gradually letters came into view, branded on the wood. They read: *Winchester Arms Co.* Using the Bowie, he prised the box open. It held a dozen unused Winchester carbines.

He spent the rest of the day digging and carrying. It was laborious work, but when he was finished the entire cache was moved to the top of the mesa, hidden in a split and covered with loose rock. He used his hands to shovel the dirt back into the hole and then he rode his horse over the place until he was satisfied the original diggers wouldn't notice the difference. Until it was too late. Gunn didn't like Comancheros.

He ate something and rode on through the night heading for the Flying D.

For the next hundred miles he travelled under cover of darkness, hiding up by day to avoid the roving bands of Comanches growing ever thicker on the ground. The horse warriors – Nemmenna, they called themselves – seemed to be on the lookout, checking the country for intruders as though guarding something. Gunn decided it must be their main camp.

Comanches, though, were not his chief concern, merely a hindrance along his vengeance trail. His quarry was Nolan, and the southerner, Christie, and they – he hoped – would be found at the Flying D.

He calculated that by now they must have reached the

spread, even allowing for the greater travelling time necessitated by the woman and the wagon. His own progress had been rapid, born of the fury of impatience consuming him, but night riding was slower and the need to stay clear of the Comanches was taking up valuable time. After three days of hiding, he allowed his hate to gain the upper hand and took the risk of travelling under the sun.

Three bucks picked up his trail on the second day. They were circling out from the main camp with no purpose in mind other than seeing what might be around. The tracks of a lone horse riding a shod pony promised some sport they hadn't really bargained on. Gleefully they urged their mustangs after the rider.

Lone Dog saw him first and screamed a war whoop, kicking his wiry pony into a headlong charge. Behind him, Tall Eagle and Pony Runner strove to outdistance their friend and count first coup on the white man.

Gunn heard the scream and glanced back. There was no cover to hand, and a fight could attract more warriors, so he rammed his heels against the gelding's ribs and gave the beast its head. The roan responded with a burst of speed that confirmed its quarter-horse ancestry, hurling itself into a long-legged gallop that carried Gun away from the pursuing Comanches. He sat low in the saddle, enjoying the sheer excitement of the wild rush, studying the ground ahead for a suitable spot to make a stand. Lone Dog and Pony Runner brought their war lances down parallel with the ground, anticipating the killing thrust they hoped to make. Tall Eagle nocked an arrow against the sinew string of his buffalo bone bow and urged his mustang up beside Lone Dog's. He tucked the single guide rein loosely under his left thigh, steering his mount with knees and heels as he drew the powerful bow.

Gunn felt the arrow go past and hunkered lower in the saddle. He reached forwards to the Winchester sheathed ahead of his right knee, and slid the carbine from the scabbard. A dry wash showed off to his left and he turned the roan towards it.

He went over the bank at full gallop, hit the sandy bottom and came out of the saddle. The velocity of the charge carried him yards down the wash and he stretched his legs, racing alongside the horse. Then he dropped the reins and ran back up the bank. Free of his weight, the gelding slowed and stopped. The reins fell, touched the sand, and the horse waited, ground-hitched.

Gunn threw himself down on the rim of the wash, lining the Winchester on the leading Comanche. He fired once and traversed the carbine, raking the Indians with .44-40 slugs.

Lone Dog saw the puff of smoke cloud his target and felt something slap his stomach. A stinging like the bite of a horse-fly nipped at his belly and he was suddenly aware of an empty feeling between his legs. Then he realised that he was in the air, his mustang charging wild before him. The ground hit him a tremendous blow and he tumbled bloodily over the sand. He tried to stand up, opening his mouth to call the runaway pony, but his throat seemed to constrict and the stinging in his midriff became a great surging pain that clouded his vision so that he grunted and fell back. He clasped his belly and felt a warmth that was wet and slightly sticky. When he lifted one hand, it was a very bright red and as he studied it he became aware of more red dripping from his mouth. He forced his body up to a sitting position, abruptly aware that he was dying. Painfully, he began to chant his death-song, but before he finished a lot more blood came from his mouth and he crumpled over into silence.

Gunn's rapid fire turned Tall Eagle away, but Pony Runner was too excited and moving too fast for anything but a head-on charge. He came over the edge of the wash with his lance pointed at Gunn's chest and a whoop bellowing from his opened mouth. To his surprise, the white man moved as fast as any Indian, hurling himself aside so that the lance passed through empty air. Pony Runner kept going, planning to rush the far bank and circle back for a second thrust.

Gunn spoiled his plan.

Rolling down the shallow decline, he came up on one knee with the Winchester against his shoulder. He fired over open sights, relying on his natural skill to hit the Comanche.

The bullet took Pony Runner in the centre of his back, directly between, and just below, his shoulder blades. It nicked a chip of bone from his spine, jerking him upright as he topped the bank. His arms shot out, rigid, to either side, his lance flying away as nerveless fingers spread wide. A hole opened in his chest as the bullet exited, tearing a gaping wound that spilled crimson froth and fragments of lung over the mustang's neck. Then Pony Runner fell backwards off the animal. He cartwheeled down the bank, his passage leaving a wide, red trail that ended at his corpse.

Before the body had stopped tumbling, Gunn was turning away, moving fast for the upper rim of the wash. An arrow thunked into the sand inches from his shoulder and he swung the carbine, squeezing the trigger. The hammer clicked on an empty magazine. He dropped the weapon, twisting sideways to grab at the Colt. The handgun was on his left hip, butt forwards for easier usage from horseback, so now it was between his stomach and the sand. As he reached across, Tall Eagle showed.

The Comanche had realised that the Winchester was empty and was coming in for the kill. He loosed a third arrow as Gunn turned, lifting the Colt. The stone arrow-head hit the cylinder, smashing the revolver out of Gunn's grasp. Tall Eagle whooped triumphantly, drawing his bow-string taught.

Gunn wasted no time thinking. Pure reflex, cat-fast and far more deadly, swung his hand over and down, reaching for the throwing knife tucked into his right moccasin. His fingers closed around the haft and his hand came up in a single clean movement that spun the knife in an underarm throw. The blade glittered briefly in the sun before imbedding itself deep in Tall Eagle's left shoulder. The Comanche grunted, dropping his bow with the arrow still nocked. He sprang to his feet, pulling a stone-tipped war club from his belt.

Gunn drew his Bowie knife, powering forwards to meet the Indian in mid charge. He saw the war club swing viciously at his skull and ducked under the blow, slashing the Bowie across Tall Eagle's ribs. The Comanche jumped back, dropping to a crouch. Gunn faced him, the knife extended at arm's length, cutting edge uppermost, needle tip level with the Indian's lower abdomen.

Tall Eagle screamed a war cry and rushed in, the club whistling through the air. Gunn moved sideways and back, avoiding the blow, letting the power of the swing pull the Comanche off balance. As Tall Eagle recovered, his opponent stepped close, cutting the knife across his right side. Before the man could use the club again. Gunn reversed his cut, hacking a second red line above the first.

The Comanche grunted and dropped to his knees, trying for a blow to the legs. Gunn jumped high over the club, coming down with his left foot kicking at Tall Eagle's shoulder. The move took the Indian by surprise and he fell back. Before he could roll away, Gunn's right foot came down on his wrist and the blond man pivoted, grinding his heel against the bone. Had the ground been harder, Tall Eagle's arm would have broken. As it was excruciating pain ran up the limb and his fingers went numb. He kicked upwards, trying to smash his feet into Gunn's ribs. The halfbreed stepped back, out of range, and grabbed one ankle. He pulled hard, flipping Tall Eagle over onto his face. Then he dropped, driving both knees into the Comanche's ribcage. Air gusted from the Indian's lungs and Gunn hooked his left hand under the man's chin. He yanked the head back, stretching the neck so that the tendons stood out in stark relief against the copper skin. And his right hand came down in a short, slashing arc. The Bowie knife cut deep into Tall Eagle's throat, severing the jugular vein, hacking through the windpipe. A scarlet fountain jetted from the wound and the Comanche made a low, gurgling noise. For a moment, his hands scrabbled against the grip on his chin, then he fell loose, his arms dangling limply by his sides.

Gunn held the body arched backwards until the flow of blood faltered and slowed and he was sure the man was dead. Then he released the near-severed head, letting Tall Eagle flop face down onto the sand.

He wiped the Bowie knife clean on the corpse's breech-clout and pushed the blade into its sheath. He pulled the throwing knife from the shoulder, wiped it, and pushed it back into his moccasin. Then he collected the fallen Colt, picked up the Winchester and thumbed a fresh load into the gate. The roan was fidgeting nervously farther up the wash, its eyes rolling as the smell of blood caught its wide-spread nostrils. Gunn walked over to it, murmuring softly until the horse calmed down again. He shoved the carbine into the saddle boot and swung astride the big gelding, glancing once at the fallen Comanches.

'There's some say the only good Indian's a dead one,' he muttered. 'But if your brothers find you, you're bad news.'

He dug his heels into the pony's ribs and galloped northwards.

CHAPTER FIVE

Nolan's reaction was instantaneous. A cavalry command in the Civil War had taught him that on open ground attack was by far the best means of defence. Now he applied the notion with desperate speed.

The Indians were coming in at full gallop, spreading to clear a field of fire as they charged what they thought was easy prey. Nolan looped his reins around the saddlehorn, smashed his boots into his horse's ribs and began to fire the Winchester. He rode headlong at the approaching Comanches, dimly aware of Christie racing alongside.

The Southerner had served his time with Jeb Stuart and there was little he didn't know about cavalry tactics. His partner's intention was obvious to him, and he followed Nolan's lead without a second thought. Triggering his own carbine from the hip, he opened his mouth and split the suddenly noisesome air with the old rebel yell.

The charge took the Comanches by surprise. They had expected the whites to falter, most likely turn back to the wagon. To find two screaming riders heading straight at them with guns blazing was an unprecedented move. Three toppled from their pad saddles with bullets through them before they were quite sure what was going on. Then the crazy whites were in amongst them, and two more Indians went down. The madmen charged through, swung their horses around and came back.

The Indians split, one group continuing the initial attack, racing for the wagon, the other turning to face the outriders.

Jack Street used a bullwhip to lash his team to full speed, shouting for Eleanor Dalton to hand him the scattergun stowed beneath the drive seat.

The Comanches closed in as she touched the gun and arrows thudded into the wagon frame. Rifles crackled, but the Indians were unused to the weapons, their aim erratic. The immediate danger was that they would kill one of the horses, dragging the whole team to a stop, and then take their time finishing off the passengers. That thought was uppermost in Jack Street's mind as he flailed his whip at the panting animals.

'Fer Chrissakes!' His voice was a frantic shout. 'Use the gun.'

Eleanor was familiar with Frontier hardware; any woman living on the Staked Plains had to be. But she was unused to shotguns. Street's weapon was a double-barrelled Meteor 10-gauge, a heavy gun at the best of times. From the seat of a bucking wagon it was doubly difficult to handle. But the choice lay between using the thing or facing death – worse, capture. She hauled the twin hammers back to full cock and forgot her dignity as she lifted one stockinged leg to brace herself against the frontboard.

A Comanche thundered alongside, fierce eyes glaring from a painted face. Eleanor looked at him and shuddered at the hate she saw. She squeezed the forward trigger.

A sound like thunder exploded around her and she pitched hard against Street as the Meteor's discharge slammed the gun back into her shoulder. The Indian's head was obscured by the black powder smoke. When it cleared the head was gone. The body still sat the pony, but where the face had been there was only a ragged stump of gory neck. Insanely, she remembered the old story of the Headless Horseman, and forced back a giggle of hysteria. The mustang kept going, pacing the racing team, but slowly the Indian's corpse shifted sideways, falling away into the roiling dust.

Another brave rode the corpse into the ground, aiming an arrow at the wagon horses. Eleanor fired again, shouting incoherently as the heavy gauge shot smashed the pony and its rider sideways in a rolling welter of bloodied limbs.

Man and beast fell directly in the path of the following riders, and three Comanches hit the bodies at full gallop. The ponies went down screaming, pitching the Indians over their heads to crash heavily onto the sand. Only one stood up.

Another warrior moved in from the side and Jack Street swung the bullwhip. The weighted lash curled around the man's face, lacerating his cheeks before the wagon's momentum pulled him off balance. His pony, sensing the shift in weight, veered to the side and the Comanche was hauled clear. He screamed as the whip tightened around his face and throat, dragging his bouncing body along behind the wagon. Then Street dropped the whip and the Indian rolled over in the dust, his tongue protruding black from between his teeth. Street dragged an ageing Navy Colt from his belt and fired methodically into the Comanches still galloping alongside.

'Shells!' Eleanor screamed. 'Where are the shells?'

'Box,' Street shouted back, steering one-handed, 'by yore feet.'

She bent over, reaching for the wooden container nailed to the boards.

It was a lucky move. For her. It meant that the arrow aimed in her direction flew close over her back. Instead of pinning her left arm to her side, it hit Jack Street below his left armpit. He screamed and dropped the Navy Colt, scrabbling at the feathered shaft sticking out from between his ribs. The guide reins were wound around his wrist, and when his arm went limp, the team yanked the leathers tight, dragging his hand forwards.

He moaned and tried to pull the arrow clear, then gave up and concentrated on guiding the team with his good hand.

A quarter mile away now, Nolan and Christie faced six Indians. Their double charge had dropped eight Comanches, but now the element of surprise was gone and they were into a running fight. Their horses were faster than the stocky mustangs, but lacked the staying power of the wiry ponies. Their carbines were empty and they were moving too fast, fighting too hard, to chance reloading. The Colts they used were inaccurate at anything other than pointblank range, so they concentrated on staying ahead of the whooping braves.

Christie's animal already sported three arrows in its rump and side, but the wounds were not serious enough to slow it. Nolan had a shaft sticking through his left arm and no time to break it off. He was bleeding, but the adrenalin pumping through his bloodstream dulled the pain and he still used his Colt whenever a target showed close enough. He shot two Comanches out of their saddles and swore when the hammer fell on an empty cylinder. A warrior came in from the side, angling a metal-headed lance for a gut thrust. Nolan slapped the pole away and drove his horse into the Indian's. The heavier animal hit the mustang like a battering ram, and the painted pony careened off, its forelegs folding. It tumbled, rolling over its rider so that his legs were crushed and he screamed as jagged shards of broken bone ripped out through the flesh.

Christie swung his gun like a club, hammering at the Indian, trying to shatter his skull with a stone hatchet. The axe glanced off his shoulder, and he kicked out, slamming his boot against the Comanche's thigh. The Indian fought to keep his balance and Christie seized the slight advantage. He swung in close, ramming the barrel of the Colt straight into the man's face. The Indian's nose shattered and blood drenched his painted chest. Instinctively, he hauled his pony away, hit a following rider, and both went down. Christie screamed the rebel yell again and began to load the Colt at full gallop.

They were slightly ahead of the Indians now, the attackers whittled down to one, who was getting second thoughts about the odds.

Christie grinned, a high-pitched giggle bursting from his lips as he realised that he held the advantage. The Comanche was carrying a Spencer repeater, but his fire was wild, inaccurate. The Southerner, in contrast, was adept with handguns, on foot or on horseback. Swinging sideways in his saddle, he allowed the Comanche to close up, felt a bullet ruffle the horse's mane, and came upright as the Indian levered a fresh shell into the repeater. He twisted, extending his arm towards the warrior, and fired twice.

The first bullet missed. The second hit the Comanche in the throat. It blew his windpipe away, breaking the vertebrae connecting shoulderblades and skull. Blood spouted from the wound and a whoop died silent on dead lips. The Indian's head jerked sideways, bouncing against his shoulders like a crazy pendulum. Then it flopped backwards, bobbing behind, and he pitched over and was gone.

Christie urged his horse onwards, bloodlust taking control of his senses. He passed Nolan at full gallop, heading straight for the Comanches chasing the wagon.

The madness communicated itself to the dark man and he drummed his heels against his horse, triggering wild shots at the Indians. None hit and he rammed the gun back into the holster, transferring his grip to the Winchester. He grasped the carbine in both hands, holding the barrel and swinging the weapon like a club. Before the Indians knew what was happening, the two men were in amongst them.

Christie emptied his revolver, killing three braves. Nolan clubbed two more from their ponies. Then the woman emptied both barrels of the Meteor into the attackers. The buckshot spread in a diamond pattern, tearing through hide war shields, skin, and bone with equal indifference. One brave lifted from his mount, most of his chest torn away by the shot, three more clutched shattered limbs and ravaged eyes. For a moment, they fell back, letting the wagon and the outriders pull ahead.

By now the team was tiring, and both Nolan's and Christie's horses were blowing hard.

The mustangs were tougher, used to the punishment of the war trail, and began to close up.

Nine Indians remained, sufficient to finish the running battle.

Jack Street was barely conscious, the arrow gouging a widening hole as his arm jerked and tugged on the reins of the wagon. Nolan could feel a creeping numbness stiffen his left arm, and blood was draining from Christie's horse as the flesh wounds pumped vital energy over its flanks. Only Eleanor Dalton remained unharmed and unhampered. Her bonnet was gone, and her blonde hair streamed in the windrush. Her face was smudged with dust and tears and spattered blood, but a fierce smile showed on her lips as she shoved a new load into the scattergun. It was almost as though she had begun to enjoy the combat.

'How far to the ranch?'

Nolan bellowed above the thunder of hooves and savage screams. He knew they couldn't last much longer.

'We're close,' Eleanor shrieked. 'If they hear the guns, Nat'll send men out.'

'He better,' grunted Nolan, looking back at the Indians. 'We ain't gonna last much longer.'

Jack Street used the lull to draw a knife. He hacked through the reins, freeing his damaged arm. As he transferred the leathers to his right hand the wagon lurched, bucking as it passed over a half-hidden rock. Street lost his balance, screamed once, and tumbled clear. Panicked, the team raced on out of control. Christie saw it happen, and swung his horse close to the rig. The animal was beginning to flag, and the Southerner coaxed its last reserves of energy to one final spurt. He forgot about Street as he reached across, grabbing the seat. Then he hauled clear of his mount, swinging on board the hurtling wagon. He snatched the loose reins and concentrated on holding the team to its mad gallop.

Street hit the ground and cartwheeled over. Stunned by the fall, and weakened by the arrow, he saw dimly that the wagon was moving fast away from him. Painfully, he climbed to his feet. And saw the Comanches.

In moments of extreme stress the human body resorts automatically to a biochemical protective system. Large quantities of adrenalin are pumped through the bloodstream, dulling pain and speeding reflexes to an abnormal degree. The adrenalin produces an effect that seems to slow time, to reduce the action around the subject to slow motion.

That effect took hold of Jack Street.

He saw the Comanches riding straight at him. He watched one of them fire a lever-action Henry, and grinned as the shot flew wide. He watched another aim a bow, and glanced down as the arrow hit him in the stomach. Then he watched two more braves level war lances at him – and wondered idly which would reach him first. He was vaguely surprised that it was the smaller of the two mustangs that covered the ground fastest, and amazed that he felt no pain when the lance went in.

It hit dead centre of his stomach, just the buckle of his leather belt. The sharp stone tip punctured the soft skin, drove on through flesh and intestines, and ripped out through his left kidney. The Comanche charged past, spinning Street around, and dragged the lance free. The second brave struck as the driver was turning. His lance tore into Street's ribs, cut through a lung, and grated on his spinal column. Street was dead, but he didn't know it. Instead, he watched the Indians go by, then turned back to watch the main group. A third brave swung a war club that ripped half the driver's scalp clear of his skull. Another planted an arrow in his back, and a third ended the affair with a Springfield carbine he had bought from Samuel Graves. The bullet hit Jack Street at pointblank range, blew most of his chest out, and knocked him five feet sideways. He sprawled on the sand, oblivious of the hooves crushing his body, and died.

His last thought was that he hadn't been paid for his driving.

As he went down for the last time, Nolan glanced back, and grinned. The Indians were slowing, wheeling away to let the wagon outdistance them. They had had enough, and – in typical Comanche fashion – were giving up to cut their losses. He let his own horse slow as Christie brought the wagon team back to control and grinned at the woman.

Up ahead a wooden sign stuck out of the ground. It was a ten-foot pine pole with a section of planking nailed to the top. Burned into the planking was a big letter *D* with three horizontal lines trailing behind the capital: it was the Flying D brand.

'I guess,' he shouted, 'that we made it.'

In the Comanche village, the Comancheros were getting impatient. Iron Knife was still absent and the two braves posted outside the entrance to the lodge allowed no-one to leave. Food had been brought to them, and blankets, but the tent was crowded and hot and beginning to smell bad. They had been cooped up all night and most of the following day, and Graves could sense the tension mounting amongst his pistoleros.

There was a whole lot of activity going on around the camp, but the Comancheros couldn't see what it was about. Instead, they heard a good deal of shouting, the reverberation of skin drums, the shriller clatter of shell rattles and the thin piping of bone flutes.

It was an eerie, ominous feeling to be conscious of the activity without knowing what it was about, and Graves didn't like it.

He liked it even less when Iron Knife appeared. The Comanche war chief was dressed in a breech-clout and feathered bonnet, the tails hanging nearly to his feet. There was no paint on his face, so the expression of anger was clearly visible.

'You bring only a few guns.' He spoke without preamble. 'Where others?'

Graves came to his feet, choosing his words carefully. He was treading a dangerous tightrope and he knew it: one word from Iron Knife and he was dead.

'They're good guns,' he said slowly, 'the kind you wanted. All repeaters.'

'Where others?' Iron Knife interrupted.

'Close,' said Graves hurriedly. 'I can show you where.'

'No.' Iron Knife shook his head. 'You stay here. The old one will show me.'

Paco swallowed hard as he realised the Comanche referred to him. He glanced at El Negro, waiting for Graves to offer some kind of lead. The renegade shrugged, keeping his dark face expressionless.

'You'll need men to handle the wagon. I can take my men back to the cache, then you can drive the guns back here.'

Iron Knife smiled. On his face it was an unnerving expression.

'No.' He spoke slowly, still smiling. 'You stay. The old one and six others will handle the guns.'

He pointed at the six pistoleros. One, a good-looking *rubio* of no more than eighteen years, lost his nerve. Mouthing an incoherent curse, he reached for his gun. As it lifted from the holster Iron Knife's right hand came up above his shoulder, swinging down with a fierce, forwards movement. The hatchet he carried flew from his grip, turning over once. It was a steel-headed axe – Graves recognised the design as one he had sold to the Comanches – and it split the pistolero's face like a ripe plum. The Colt dropped unused from the youngster's fingers, and he stood for a moment with the two halves of his shattered head spilling blood over his boots. Then he fell down.

'The old one and *five* others,' said Iron Knife calmly.

He stepped forwards, reaching down to tug the axe free. Behind him, four warriors crowded into the tepee with rifles covering the Comancheros.

'Wait here,' ordered the chief, 'we leave soon.'

When he returned he was in full paint, carrying the Winchester Graves had given him. Paco and the remaining pistoleros followed him to the wagons. They were allowed to keep their weapons, but the Indians surrounding them made it obvious that any attempt to escape would be useless. Reluctantly, the Comancheros mounted up and rode out.

They reached the mesa with sunset drawing close, and Paco pointed to the spot where they had buried the guns.

'Dig,' Iron Knife ordered.

Grumbling, the pistoleros took spades from the wagon and began to shift dirt. They moved the topsoil and Paco gasped. The sound was halfway between surprise and fear: the hidden crates were gone. Urgently, the Mexicans cleared more dirt, refusing to admit the inevitable. They scooped a trench over twelve inches deep before Paco turned to the Indians.

'*Jefe,*' he said quietly, 'they are gone.'

Iron Knife's face stayed impassive, his cold, black eyes studying the Mexican's. Paco fidgeted nervously, fingering the rosary at his neck. Then Iron Knife, still staring directly at him, said something in the Comanche tongue. The pistoleros didn't need a translation to understand what the words meant. They went for their guns.

The Indians were ready. Rifles barked and the Mexicans went down riddled with arrows and gunshot wounds. Paco fell to his knees, mumbling a prayer, his eyes tight shut.

He heard the guns fall silent, smelled the reek of cordite, and opened his eyes.

Iron Knife was smiling. Like a wolf. And his carbine was pointing straight at Paco's face.

'Why you lie?'

'I didn't!' Paco's voice was a terrified howl. He had expected to die: to find himself still alive was more than his nerves could take. 'I swear it! On my mother's grave, *jefe,* I swear the guns were here.'

'Not now.'

Iron Knife walked his pony close to the Mexican, nudging his chin with the Winchester so that Paco stared up at him.

'They were here.' Tears coursed down the old man's cheeks. 'We buried them here. They must be here.'

He dropped on all fours scrabbling desperately at the sand, willing the crates to appear.

Iron Knife grunted something and Little Buffalo unshipped a rawhide lariat from his saddle. He swung the loop over Paco's head, jerking it tight around the grizzled neck. He backed his pony, dragging Paco forward so that he fell face down in the sand, the rawhide digging into his skin. Iron Knife issued more orders, and a brave climbed onto the wagon, slipping the brake.

'Stand up,' said Iron Knife, harshly. 'We go back. Talk with the Black One.'

He turned his pony in the direction of the camp and Paco stood up. Little Buffalo followed the war chief, heeling his mount to a trot that drew the lariat taut behind him. Paco began a stumbling run. It was difficult to keep up: his high-heeled boots were made for riding, not footwork, and the heavy spurs he wore snagged on the rough ground. Every time he fell down the rawhide noose tightened on his windpipe, cutting off his air, and he gagged, choking until Little Buffalo slowed enough for him to draw closer, slackening the lariat.

A revolver still hung at Paco's waist, but he never thought of using it. His entire concentration was focussed solidly on staying upright and alive; the unpleasant possibilities of his future were forgotten in the tortured need to keep moving without choking to death.

By the time they reached the Indian village, Paco's tongue was hanging out of his mouth and his feet were raw hunks of blistered flesh.

Little Buffalo halted outside the big lodge and dropped the lariat. Paco collapsed, his hands tugging madly at the noose. He had it loosened enough to fill his burning lungs when two braves picked him up and threw him into the tent. He landed on his stomach and lay there, panting like an old, sick dog.

'What in the hell happened?' Graves' voice was urgent. 'Paco! Where are the others?'

'Dead.' The Mexican had trouble shaping the words. 'All dead.'

'Why fer Chrissakes?' Graves shook the old man. 'What went on out there?'

'Gone,' Paco mumbled. 'Guns gone.'

'Oh, sweet Jesus!' Graves was scared now. 'Tell me.'

Hernando slopped water into Paco's wide-opened mouth, his lips moving in a silent prayer. Graves waited until Paco had swallowed, then cradled his shoulders, pulling the noose clear of his neck.

'What happened, Paco?'

'We got to the mesa.' Paco spoke slowly, forming the words carefully around a swollen tongue. 'And began to dig. The guns weren't there. They were gone. Iron Knife told his men to kill the others. They walked me back.'

'They can't be gone!' Graves refused to believe it.

'They are gone, *jefe*.' Paco swallowed more water. 'Like the desert ate them up.'

'Fuck!' Graves snarled. 'Where the hell does that leave us?'

'Dead.' John Bear answered the question. 'Iron Knife will kill us for cheating him. Slowly.'

He hunkered down, watching Paco with stoic indifference, knowing what he could expect and accepting the inevitability of painful death. The others, lacking his Indian calm, began to talk escape. They had five sidearms and three knives between them; Graves carried a hideaway derringer in his boot, but he was keeping that to himself. And there was still a slim chance he could talk his way out.

He got an opportunity to try when Iron Knife reappeared.

'You lie to me, Black One,' said the Comanche. 'There were no guns.'

Graves thought fast. 'We buried 'em there. If they ain't in the ground, it has to be because someone found 'em.'

'There were no guns,' repeated Iron Knife.

'I can get more.' Graves talked as fast as he was thinking. 'I'll go back to Quintana and bring you more.'

'If you go, why you come back?' Iron Knife looked at the negro with contempt.

'Keep the others,' said Graves, fast. 'Hold them as hostages.'

John Bear spat in disgust, and Iron Knife's lips curled in a sneer.

'Man who give friends up so easy is worth nothing.' His hand made a chopping gesture: dismissal. 'Your word not mean much, Black One.'

'The gold,' faltered Graves, 'you keep half. Pay me the rest when I come back with the guns.'

Iron Knife snorted. 'We only get half the guns. Why give you any gold? Man with gold ride far, not look back.'

The logic was irrefutable and Graves felt his arguments crumble to nothing. Then the Comanche smiled.

'He go.' Paco groaned as he realised that Iron Knife was pointing in his direction. 'He take message to Quintana: your friends send guns, or you die.' He laughed, filling the lodge with an ugly sound. 'Tonight I show you how you die. Tomorrow the old one can go.'

He called something in Comanche and the warriors at his back seized the Comancheros, stripping them of their weapons. The only gun they didn't find was Graves' derringer. Then they herded the prisoners from the tent, out to the centre of the village.

The camp was built in a series of circles, the tepees growing larger and brighter painted the closer they got to the centre. There, an open space about one hundred yards across was illuminated by numerous fires. The flames shone on row after row of painted faces, all turned excitedly towards the prisoners. Pushed on by their guards, Graves and his men stumbled through the massed ranks of the Indians, Enrico and Hernando supporting the limping Paco between them. They stopped when they saw the scaffolds.

Lodge poles, each one about fifteen feet high, were imbedded in the sand to form two tripods. They were in clear sight of all the Comanches, and two big fires burned close by.

John Bear sucked in his breath, knowing what was coming.

Iron Knife grunted and Paco fell to the ground as the braves seized Enrico and Hernando, dragging them towards the poles. The Mexicans struggled, yelling, as rawhide was lashed tight around their wrists and slung over the apex of both scaffolds. Whooping warriors tugged eagerly on the hide ropes, hauling the renegades off the ground. When the rawhides were fastened down, the two men dangled a good four feet up in the air. More Indians piled wood and buffalo chips beneath their feet, then Iron Knife nodded and the fires were lit.

The Mexicans screamed as they felt the flames singe their boots. They were not hurting yet, but the anticipation of pain was sufficient to render them near-hysterical, and they twisted, jerking wildly on the ropes. Their contortions served only to swing them back and forth above the licking, red tongues, and gradually their boots and chaps began to smoulder. Flickering sparks darted over their legs, the stained leather of their pants blackening as the acrid smell of burning lay heavy on the night air. They seemed to run on the flames, their legs pumping hopelessly as they tried to lift themselves above the pain.

'Watch carefully, Black One,' Iron Knife murmured. 'If the guns do not arrive, you will die slower than this.'

Graves shuddered.

From the ground, close by his feet, Paco looked away from the horrible spectacle, up towards El Negro.

'*Jefe*,' he said quickly, 'I don't think your insurance policy payed off.'

From the ridge above the depression containing the camp a lone figure lay belly down on the sand, watching.

Matthew Gunn had circled round after killing the three

Comanches, hiding his back trail. The signs he had read told him he was close enough to the Comanche village to risk a minor detour and check out the size of the gathering. Like the other sign, it confirmed his first impression: there were more horse warriors collected there than the Staked Plains had seen in years. The presence of the wagons and the Mexicans told him where the guns he had shifted came from, and he grinned as he guessed the two men dancing on the fires were being tortured as a result of his actions. Their suffering was no concern of his, though he was grateful for the diversion it created, holding the Comanches to the camp.

The screams echoed as he moved silently back to his horse, reaching a new pitch of frenzy.

'That's one problem about Indian trading,' he grinned. 'Louse up a deal and things can get hot.'

CHAPTER SIX

Eleanor Dalton greeted her husband like a dutiful wife.

Nolan couldn't help grinning as he watched her wrap her arms around Nathaniel's shoulders and kiss him like she meant it. It was a performance worthy of a St. Louis actress, and it pulled the wool firmly over Dalton's eyes. As firmly as the cuckold's horns she had put on his head. When the man drew away, one arm still resting over his wife's back and turned to Nolan, the dark man made the grin look like approval of the reunion.

The woman had spilled the story of their journey in a fast, nervous narrative that didn't give Dalton a chance to say anything. The only part she left out was how she had been sleeping with Nolan, and now her two escorts were big men around the Flying D.

To hear Eleanor tell it, they had fought their way through the entire Comanche nation.

Her husband shook their hands and thanked them fervently, inviting them to stay as long as they wished.

'Could be you'd have trouble leavin' anyway,' he said. 'The Comanch' bin' actin' up real bad lately. I lost better'n fifty head, an' they hit the ranch once.'

'That so?' Nolan injected a note of sympathy into his voice. 'You got any ideas why?'

Dalton shook his head, ushering them into the main building. The Flying D was a solid-looking place built for protection rather than fancy architecture. The ranch-house itself was a squat, one-storey structure of stone and plaster, Mexican-style tiles covering the roof. It was built around a central courtyard with a spring supplying drinking water and an inner veranda, shade. The outward-facing walls were plastered white, with narrow windows covering all four approaches and a heavy wood door the only way in. It was like a fort.

Off to the side, a timber bunkhouse flanked a big barn with a smithy set under a lean-to. A tall windmill pumped water to a trough beside the barn, and doubled as a look-out post. The whole set-up was fenced around with heavy planking some seven feet high.

Dalton offered them whisky and chairs while Eleanor disappeared across the courtyard to change, and the men settled down to discussing the Indian problem.

'I cain't figger it,' Dalton answered Nolan's question. 'We had trouble when we came into the territory, but the injuns bin peaceable the past couple years. A beef or two was all they took. Now all of a sudden they're spoilin' fer a fight.'

He paused, topping up their glasses.

'Like I said, they hit the ranch. Come right in close. They ain't tried that since we built it. Thing was, they had guns.'

'That ain't unusual,' Christie pointed out. 'They always got a few guns.'

'Not like this,' Dalton shook his head. 'I never seen 'em carryin' so many before. Repeaters too. Ain't often you see Comanches usin' Spencers, let alone Winchesters. They had plenty o' ammunition, too.'

'They was usin' repeaters when they jumped us,' said Nolan thoughtfully.

'I reckon there's a war brewin',' Dalton added. 'They're pickin' up repeaters from the Comancheros an' workin' themselves up fer a big sweep.'

'Ain't the Army doin' anything?' Christie asked.

'Ain't much it can do,' retorted Dalton. 'Ain't more'n five forts to cover the whole o' Texas. Hell, there's Fort Worth coverin' the entire territory from the old Shawnee Trail to the Sabine an' the border. Concho's nigh on two hundred miles away, an' Fort Quitman's busy watchin' New Mexico fer Apache trouble.'

He poured more whisky.

'What's that leave?' He took a drink and answered his own question. 'Fort Davis an' Fort Stockton got the responsibility. Trouble is, they ain't got the men. The cavalry's spread so damn' thin we don't see a patrol more'n once a month if we're lucky. An' if there's a flare-up someplace else we're on our own.'

'You got the Texas Rangers,' Christie suggested.

'Yeah,' nodded Dalton, 'but they got their own troubles. Ain't so many o' them, an' the State's big enough to keep 'em pretty busy.'

While he spoke, Nolan was studying him, weighing up the rancher. Nathaniel Dalton was a tired-looking man with permanent wrinkles worried into his forehead, and crow's feet lines that weren't all due to the sun spreading out from his tired eyes. Once, he had been a powerful figure, standing straight and broad-shouldered. Now he slumped, his shoulders stooped under the burden of too much hard work and too much worry. Nolan wondered what he'd do if he knew his wife was unfaithful. When the time was right he'd have to tell Dalton and find out.

For now, though, he was content to listen.

'Fact is,' Dalton was saying, 'that I'm kinda glad to see you two. I know you done what Eleanor hired you for, an' I owe you for that, but I'd like to put another proposition to you.'

Again he filled their glasses, as though hoping the liquor would persuade them.

'From what Eleanor told me, you're both pretty handy with a gun. Right now I can use some help in that department. How'd you feel about stayin' on fer a while? I'll pay well.'

Christie shrugged, waiting for Nolan to speak. The dark man grinned, turning his green-eyed gaze full on Dalton's tired face.

'Sure. We'll stay around fer a spell.'

Eleanor chose that moment to reappear wearing a crisp calico dress that outlined the contours of her figure in a way that made Nolan wonder how they could arrange some more time together. Her golden hair was piled up around her head, emphasising her big eyes and wide mouth, and her smile was both secretive and demure.

'Honey,' Nathaniel turned, grinning as she placed a hand on his shoulder, 'these fellers have agreed to stay on fer a bit.'

'How pleasant. I'm sure Mr. Nolan and Mr. Christie will be most helpful. We became quite good friends on the journey here.'

She looked directly at Nolan as she said it, her face straight, betraying nothing. Nolan grinned back.

'We sure can use two extra guns,' said Nathaniel.

'Yes,' agreed Eleanor, 'and Mr. Nolan is very handy with his weapon. As is Mr. Christie.'

Nolan kept the smile fixed across his mouth and Jude Christie fought hard to surpress a snigger.

Dalton rose to his feet, explaining that he had to check something with his foreman, and left Eleanor to show his new-found hands to their rooms. Still playing the part of the good wife, she lead the way out to the veranda. The sleeping quarters were on the far side of the courtyard, and she showed Christie into one room before taking Nolan on to the next. She went inside with him.

'How did you manage that?' She sounded excited.

'Easy,' grinned Nolan, pulling her towards him. 'Yore old man wants gun talent. We supply it.'

'And you know what I want,' breathed Eleanor, kissing him hard.

Yeah, thought Nolan, *I know. But will you pay the price I'm asking*?

Gunn rode away from the Comanche village slowly, taking care to keep the gelding quiet. Now that he had an idea what was happening, the Comanches were of no more interest. He had seen the gathering, and the paint, and knew that the tribes were preparing for all-out war. It wasn't his problem, except that it might interfere with his plans for Nolan and Christie. The Flying D was close enough to make itself the obvious target for the Indians' first attack, so he aimed to reach the ranch and kill the two men before the Comanches jumped them.

After that he could leave Texas to heal its own wounds and head back to New Mexico.

He found a sheltered gulley some time before dawn and made dry camp. He wanted to be fresh for the confrontation, so he settled down to sleep for a while.

Hernando and Enrico took a long time dying. Most of the night. But after a few hours, their screams died away to choking moans, and then to silence. When they stopped kicking and just hung over the fires the Comanches got bored and began to drift away. Iron Knife ordered the three remaining Comancheros lashed to stakes, and they spent the remainder of the night crouched uncomfortably on the ground, their arms dragged back behind them.

Graves got a little sleep around dawn, but as the sun came up the yapping of the camp dogs woke him. They were fighting over the corpses, jumping high to tear chunks of charred flesh from the dangling legs.

John Bear seemed to take it all philosophically. He had said nothing since being taken from the lodge, just watched his companions die with dark, expressionless eyes.

Graves hated him for his calm almost as much as he envied it.

Paco passed the night mumbling prayers. They did him little good because in the morning he was the first to be untied. Two braves cut the bonds holding him and dragged him towards the glowing embers of the central fire.

Paco stopped praying and began to scream, but one of the

warriors shoved a wad of old leather into his mouth and the Mexican became fully occupied with breathing around the gag.

Iron Knife appeared, wrapped in a red blanket against the dawn chill, and faced Graves.

'Tell the old one that if he fails to deliver the message you will die.' The war chief smiled evilly. 'If the guns are not here by the time the moon grows small you will die. Tell him that.'

Graves repeated the message, adding a heart-felt plea of his own. Paco nodded, his eyes wide, and the negro hoped the old man had more loyalty than his boss.

Iron Knife waited until he was sure his words were passed on. Then he drew a heavy-bladed knife. Four Indians turned Paco on his face, yanking his arms and legs out in a spreadeagle. Iron Knife stooped, slashing the tendons in Paco's calves. The Mexican choked on his gag. Iron Knife studied his work appreciatively, then hacked off Paco's thumbs. A squaw appeared and slapped crude bandages over the wounds. Then the Comanches lifted Paco onto his horse.

Iron Knife reached up and took the gag from his mouth.

'Ride fast, old one.' He smiled as he said it. 'Before long the black poison will start to rot you and you will die alone. Take the message and you might live.'

He laughed as Paco rode out of the camp.

CHAPTER SEVEN

Matthew Gunn saw the rider coming and hauled the Winchester clear of the boot as he turned his horse off the trail. He halted in the cover of some big saguaros and watched the man with interest. He was a Mexican, to judge from the big sombrero and tight, concho-studded pants. And he was hurt.

It looked as though he was having trouble staying on the horse.

When he came level with Gunn's position, the halfbreed could see why: the man's hands were bandaged and his legs badly gashed. From the way his feet dangled limp in the stirrups, Gunn guessed that the tendons were severed. Holding the Winchester pointed forwards, he rode out of cover.

'*Hola.*' His greeting was casual. 'You're hurt.'

Paco looked up, blinking through the pain that clouded his vision. He saw a man in American-style clothes and smiled gratefully. The rider was obviously friendly: he wasn't a Comanche and that fact alone meant he was either a hand off some local ranch or a scout for the Army or the Texas Rangers. No-one else would risk crossing the Staked Plains alone – except Comancheros, and Graves' outfit, Paco knew, was the only one out right now.

'*Si,*' he whispered, 'I am hurt pretty bad.'

'What happened?' The man sounded friendly enough, but for some reason he made no move to help.

'Comanches,' Paco announced dramatically, 'they tortured me.'

He had no intention of letting the stranger know that he was a Comanchero. Selling guns to the Indians was a hanging offence in Texas, worse even than horse stealing. He had already concocted a story of innocent *vaqueros* seeking work in America, only to be jumped by murderous savages.

'And let you go?' The man sounded doubtful.

'I escaped,' added Paco in a hurry. 'We were looking for work, my friends and me. The Comanches jumped us. They tortured two of us last night. I managed to get free, but there are two more still held captive. I am seeking help.'

He shuddered dramatically.

'Where are you from?'

Gunn smiled, not believing any of it. The man who broke free of a Comanche camp was gifted with more luck than anyone had a right to own. The man who could climb onto a horse with his hamstrings cut and useless hands was possessed of more strength than this oldster.

'I don't believe you,' he said evenly.

'*Que es?*' Paco was suddenly worried. 'I swear it's the truth. I must fetch help for my friends. It's lucky I met you.'

Gunn shook his head. 'I'll tell you what you are: a Comanchero.'

Paco spluttered, shaking his own head in violent negation.

'You were bringing guns to the big camp,' continued the man, who did, Paco now saw, bear a curious resemblance to an Indian. 'You buried some of them. At the foot of a mesa.'

'You!' Paco's eyes grew wide with shock and angry realisation. 'It was you! You found them and shifted them. You bastard! You know what you did?'

'Sure,' said Gunn, amused by the Comanchero's wrath. 'I spoiled a deal for you. I guess it upset your Comanche friends.'

'They slaughtered us,' snarled Paco. 'Raul, Luis ... Hernando, Enrico, over the fires ... Me. Do you know what they did to me?'

His voice rose to a hysterical shriek and he raised one hand, tearing at the bandages with his teeth. He spat the dirty rags away and held the arm out in front of him. The thumb was severed at the lower joint, where it attaches to the hand. The blood had begun to congeal, but the violent removal of the cloth had re-opened the wound and dark blood welled in pulsing globules, dripping onto the sand.

'They cut off my thumbs!' Paco screamed. 'They finished me! I can't hold a gun anymore. I can't control a horse. I'm finished.'

'It's not your lucky day, is it?' Gunn said quietly. And triggered the Winchester.

The bullet solved Paco's problems. It hit his chest directly above the heart, shattered a rib that turned it slightly so that it tore out only half the ventricle, and emerged beneath his left shoulderblade. Its force lifted him from the saddle, blowing him bodily through the air, over the horse's rear. He fell heavily onto the ground, his mutilated hands spread wide.

Almost immediately, flies began to gather around the wounds.

Gunn slid the Winchester back into the scabbard and glanced round at Paco's horse. The animal, spooked by the shot, was running wild towards the south. Gunn let it go. He didn't need a spare horse, and it would be more trouble than it was worth trying to catch it. He couldn't be certain why the Comanches had let the old man go, but he suspected it had something to do with the hidden weapons. If he was right, the remaining Comancheros had a nasty shock coming.

He grinned and rode on.

Iron Knife was less concerned about the missing shipment of guns than he showed. He had already succeeded in gathering the largest force of Nemmenna his people had ever seen. Usually, the tribes followed their own ways, living independently of one another, coming together only to trade or to arrange marriages. The magic dream he had been gifted with nearly one of the white man's years ago was now taking shape. The Nemmenna came together under his leadership, their purpose to clear the buffalo grounds of central Texas of the troublesome whites. Iron Knife had worked hard for that.

The guns he had bought with looted gold, taken from stage coaches and miners, burned-out ranches and solitary travellers, were sufficient to equip most of his warriors. More would come when they took the war trail.

The vision he had seen in the medicine tent had told him the time was come. For seven days, he had fasted, breathing the dream smoke as the shaman chanted the ritual words around his sweating body. He had sacrificed his best horse, and the gods of his people had been pleased.

In the dream he had seen many of the fast-firing guns, heard the sound of a great battle. He had seen bloody scalps hanging from the war lances, and felt the heat of burning ranches. Then the dream had shown him the plains thick with buffalo and the tents of his people and he had known that the gods smiled upon him and that the Nemmenna would be mighty upon the land.

He had emerged from the medicine lodge gaunt and hungry, his face hollowed and his ribs prominent beneath his skin. But his eyes still held the memory of the vision and he had known the time was upon him.

Now his riders carried word to the scattered groups not come to the gathering place of the dream, and he knew that soon the Nemmenna would drive the whites from the hunting grounds.

The news that Lone Dog, Pony Runner and Tall Eagle, three of his finest warriors, were dead had angered him. That the tracks of their killer went towards the ranch of the man called Dalton persuaded him to make that his first target. That Graves had failed to bring all the promised guns irritated him, but did not alter his plans. The hidden guns might be replaced if the old one lived long enough to deliver the message; if not, then Graves and the halfbreed would provide sport for the women.

Strong in his dream-power, Iron Knife summoned his chiefs and outlined the gods-given order of battle.

Simultaneously, the Comanches attacked the targets chosen by the war chief.

The Wells-Fargo stage heading west to El Paso was ambushed that afternoon. The driver, guard, and all five passengers were killed, scalped and looted. The way-stations built between the Red River and the Pecos were reduced to rubble, and nine lonely homesteads burned to the ground. A patrol of four Texas Rangers put up a running fight before the Texicans died, and the Flying D got the worse Indian attack Nathaniel Dalton had ever seen.

The Comanches came out of a clear afternoon. It was the hottest day the Staked Plains had suffered in all that long, hot summer, and Dalton was congratulating himself on busting a gut digging reliable wells when the look-out posted atop the windmill started to holler. At first Dalton thought the cowboy must have sighted a mirage. Then he saw the dust cloud and ran for the smithy. He grabbed the hammer strung beside the warning bell and sounded the alarm.

He had seven men around the main building, with Nolan, Christie and the Mexican cook inside the ranch house. Counting Eleanor as one gun, that gave him twelve people in all. The look-out, who was up there because his eye-sight was better than most, calculated around one hundred Comanches coming their way.

Dalton got his men inside the ranch building and set to forting up. The hands still out on the range would have to look after themselves. If they were still alive.

Inside the fortress-like building the window shutters were going down. They were made of two-inch thick imported oak, dense enough to stop a bullet and hung on steel hinges. The main door was oak, reinforced with metal bands, and held in place with a massive cross-bar. The walls of the ranch house were foot-thick stone that would take a cannon to breach. The defenders had a supply of fresh water from the spring, and the cook's storehouse held enough meat and canned goods to feed them for a month. It was a pity to lose the horses and the pigs that were penned behind the barn, but that couldn't be helped.

What counted now was staying alive.

He opened the bureau drawer in the main living-room and grabbed the key to the armoury. Since building the place, he had always kept a supply of carbines and handguns, together with plenty of ammunition, in a locked room. Eleanor had sometimes laughed at his precautions, telling him he was overly cautious. She wasn't laughing now.

Dalton saw that the two new men were already set up by the windows to either side of the main door, their Winchesters poked through the firing ports and opened cartons of shells in easy reach by their feet. He left them, detailing his cowhands to the remaining three walls. He assigned two men, and the cook, to filling buckets against the chance of fire and set Eleanor to preparing bandages.

Then the Flying D settled down to the hardest part: the waiting.

The dust cloud came closer and shapes began to emerge. Dalton sucked in his breath when he saw the war band. Even with the stockpiled supplies it was going to be a long, hard fight.

The Indians halted just out of range, watching the ranch like buzzards waiting for a sick cow to go down. Inside, the rooms were cool and dim, and very quiet. No-one was talking as the defenders waited for the Comanches to make their move. For what seemed like a long time, they sat their ponies in silence, painted faces studying the building.

Then the front ranks of horsemen opened and two men came forwards. There was something strange about them. They sat heavy in their saddles and they looked like white men. A Comanche struck the two horses with a quirt, and they broke into a startled gallop. As they approached the ranch house they slowed, snickering nervously, and turned towards the corral.

'Oh my God!' Dalton gasped, recognition adding furrows to his brow. 'That's Charlie and Bob.'

'*Was*,' corrected Nolan.

The two cowhands were dead. Crude frames held them upright on their horses, rawhide held hands and legs in position. Their chests were bare, criss-crossed with a tracery of cuts, blackened by the fires built on their stomachs. Their jaws gaped open, holding the organs stuffed into their mouths, and their eyes stared sightlessly: the upper lids had been cut away.

Nolan turned to Christie, nodding. They fired together and the horses dropped, spilling their macabre burdens.

Dalton choked on his own bile.

'Least they'll slow the charge,' murmured Nolan, staring out at the Indians.

Then hell broke loose and visited itself on the Flying D.

There was a great yammering scream that seemed to go on and on as the Comanches hurled themselves into a wild gallop. With the precision of well-drilled cavalry, they charged forwards in two columns, thundering head on at the ranch house. As they came within firing range the columns peeled to right and left, the Indians turning in two wide circles. It was the Comanche Wheel, the warriors galloping close enough to shoot, then swinging away out of range. It meant that individual horsemen presented only fleeting targets before they were gone into the dust, circling round for a fresh attack.

Dalton yelled for extra men to man the rifle ports of the main room: for the moment, the attack was concentrated on the front of the building. The place grew acrid with the stink of cordite, and despite the cool, men began to sweat as they levered Winchesters and Spencers with an energy that became automatic.

The Comanches raised a great cloud of billowing dust that drifted over the ranch, prickling at eyes already smarting from the gunsmoke, clogging throats and blocking nostrils.

Then, abruptly, they pulled back.

Slowly, the dust settled and Nolan began a head count. No-one inside was hurt, but seven Indians stretched on the sand. The remainder grouped out of range, then broke up into five bands. Four circled the building, commencing an attack on all four sides. The fifth converged on the corrals, driving the horses clear. Dalton cursed as smoke began to flood from the barn and bunkhouse. Scoured dry by wind and sun, the wooden buildings blazed fast, and before long they were reduced to piles of smouldering ash. Then the Indians stampeded the horse herd straight at the ranch.

The fear-crazed animals galloped headlong for the building, splitting at the last moment to thunder around the walls.

On all four sides, the Indians used the diversion to get close.

Nolan bellowed a warning as a rifle barrel poked inwards. He pulled aside as the gun went off, then stuck his own Winchester into the face that suddenly appeared at the opening. The skull disentegrated and the Comanche sprawled back. Christie saw one of the wounded braves crawling closer and shot him, then – methodically – put bullets through the other 'corpses'. Three of them screamed and twitched as his shots hit, and he giggled, pulling back to reload.

Dalton sent a man to check for casualties and began to curse again when he heard that two cowboys were dead, shot at point-blank range through the gun ports, and one more badly hurt.

The four groups continued to ride the wheels, maintaining a constant rain of bullets and arrows that kept the defenders dodging to avoid the stray shots ricochetting around the interior of the ranch.

The fifth group pulled back and began to light fires.

Suddenly the riders drew away and the flaming arrows started to fall. Nolan and Christie dropped four of the archers, but the others hauled back the strings of their powerful buffalo bows, angling shafts wrapped around with inflammable material upwards at the sky. The arrows rose high, their passage goading the flames to incandescence, and they arced above the walls, falling on the roof and courtyard.

The Mexican cook groaned and fell, dropping his water bucket as a shaft pierced his back. He screamed when he felt the flames and rolled over in a desperate attempt to douse the fire. He put out the flames, but his gyrations rammed the arrow deep into a lung and he coughed blood and died.

The arrows that struck the roof glanced off the tiles, but inside the courtyard the wood-roofed veranda began to burn, drawing more men away from the gun ports to fight the spreading blaze.

'How long do you think they'll keep it up?' Dalton rejoined Nolan and Christie in the main room.

'Can't say,' shrugged Nolan. 'An injun'll fight until he figgers he's fought enough, then he'll quit. But there ain't no way of tellin' when he'll decide he's had his fill. They could keep this up until we run outta ammunition. They could quit tonight.'

'Jesus,' muttered Dalton. It was a prayer, rather than blasphemy.

'Thing is to keep whittlin' them down,' grunted Christie. 'Ain't that right Nolan?'

The dark man growled an affirmative reply and shot a Comanche off his pony. He crossed the room, helping himself to Dalton's whisky.

'They'll kill us,' he said cynically, 'or we'll kill them. It's that simple.'

The attack went on until dark, then the Comanches fell back and the defenders got a breathing space. Around midnight, Dalton came to Nolan with a plan. The rancher appeared to regard the dark man as an authority on Indian fighting, and seemed grateful to share his responsibilities with Nolan. To the scalp hunter it sounded desperate, but as it involved someone else's life, he went along with it.

One of Dalton's hands was a Texicano, the son of an American woman. He claimed to know the territory better than most, and reckoned he could make his way through the surrounding Indians without being spotted. Nolan didn't give much for his chances, but when the boy – he was no more than eighteen – insisted he could get through to fetch help, Nolan shrugged and agreed to the idea.

The boy was called Johnny Riley and he slipped out through an opened window in the early hours of the morning.

Fifty minutes later he began to scream.

He kept screaming all through the night, his voice rising higher and higher, reaching peaks of frenzy that kept the people inside the ranch awake as they listened, wondering what the Comanches were doing to the kid.

In the morning they found out.

Johnny Riley was still alive, though he would have been better off dead. The Comanches had worked on him throughout the dark hours, and as the sun rose they lashed his mutilated body to a framework of poles and left him hanging in the clear sight of the ranch. He was naked, hurting and bleeding, and every so often he opened what was left of his mouth and howled like a wounded coyote.

The defenders listened to him for an hour, then the strain got too much and Christie grabbed one of Dalton's spare guns. It was a big Sharps .50 buffalo rifle with twice the range of the Winchesters. Christie needed it: Johnny Riley was over one thousand yards away.

The Southerner opened the breech and shoved a cartridge in. Resting the heavy barrel on a window ledge, he pulled the hammer back and sighted on Johnny's chest. He took a deep breath and let it out slow and easy as his finger tightened on the trigger. The Sharps went off with a sound like a close-range cannon. Johnny seemed to jump back against the poles, and the entire framework collapsed, raising an angry shout from the Comanches.

'Nice shot, Jude,' grinned Nolan.

'Yeah,' Christie answered, 'maybe now we'll get some peace.'

'My God.' Eleanor Dalton looked troubled by their indifference. 'How can you be so casual?'

'Ma'am,' Nolan said softly, his voice cutting through the stillness in the room, 'Jude done that fool boy a favour. He ain't hurtin' no more now.'

'Fool boy?' Eleanor queried. 'He was trying to save our lives. Is that foolish?'

'He didn't stand a hope in hell,' grunted Nolan. 'There ain't anyone gonna get through them injuns.'

'But you let him go.' The woman studied her lover's cold face with startled eyes. 'If you thought that, why did you let him go?'

Nolan shrugged. 'Guess there mighta been a faint chance. Leastways now we know where we stand.'

Eleanor turned away, shaking her head in bewildered despair. She began to wonder about Nolan.

Then she forgot her doubts and concentrated on loading the rifles as the Indians attacked again.

The man called Gunn watched the Comanches from the cover of a buffalo wallow a few thousand yards off to the side. He had been there since just after dawn, and had seen Johnny Riley's suffering and Christie's mercy shot. He was mildly interested in the Comanche tactics, comparing them with the war skills of his own people. The Chiricahuas would have avoided a frontal assault, deeming it too hazardously careless against a position so easily defended. No, they would have moved close in the night, using the darkness and the fatigue of the whites to get up against the walls, onto the roof. After that it would have been easy.

The Comanches, though, were horse warriors. They lived and died on their ponies, and they had little taste for fighting on foot.

That, and the fort-like construction of the Flying D, gave the men inside a powerful advantage. For the time being. But time, Gunn knew, would be the telling factor. There were close on a hundred Indians surrounding the ranch; the defenders couldn't hope to hold out indefinitely. And when the Comanches closed in, Nolan and Christie would die along with the others.

It presented Gunn with a difficult problem.

If he tried to help the whites, the Indians would fall on him, overwhelming him by sheer weight of numbers. If he stood by, playing it safe, the men he hunted would be taken from him. He weighed alternatives in his mind, and an idea came. It was a long shot, and dangerous as it was long; but it was all he could think of. Carefully, he began to make his preparations, working methodically through the day, waiting for nightfall when he planned to act.

Inside the ranch house, Eleanor Dalton wiped tears from her smarting eyes and fetched another bucket to the cowhands fighting the fires that threatened to take a hold on the interior.

Nathaniel dragged a fresh keg of shells from the armoury, wondering how much longer his supplies would last.

Nolan used his Winchester with automatic precision. His face was calm, the mouth set in a thin, tight line. Only the cold blaze of his green eyes betrayed the anger he felt.

Christie worked his own carbine with equally lethal skill. His blond hair was filthy with dust and smoke, his face a grimy mask. But his blue eyes were alive with pure enjoyment, and every time he dropped a Comanche, he giggled.

CHAPTER EIGHT

Clouds did their best to hide the moon and Gunn used all the cover he could find to get close to the Comanches. He moved silently, slipping from shadow to shadow the way old Sees-The-Fox had taught him. He used rocks and mesquite scrub to hide himself, bellying over the sand when he hit an open stretch, and he reached the edge of the horse herd without being seen.

The mustangs shifted nervously, and Gunn froze, waiting for them to become accustomed to his presence. In a way, it was lucky there were so many Comanches. Had the band been only a normal raiding party, the warriors would have slept with their animals hitched to wrists or ankles. The size of the war party made that impossible, so the beasts were hobbled under the care of scattered nightguards. Gunn drew his Bowie knife and waited for the nearest guard to draw close.

The man held a lever-action Spencer in his folded arms and looked bored. The expression was fixed forever on his face when Gunn killed him.

The halfbreed came out from amongst the ponies on noiseless moccasins. His left arm circled the Comanche's neck, dragging the chin up and back as a raised knee hit the base of his spine, bending him over. Then Gunn's knife cut across his throat and he died.

The incident took no more than a few seconds and when it was ended Gunn draped the Comanche's blanket around his shoulders and busied himself with the small bundles he had made during the day. Each one consisted of a square of material torn from a shirt and knotted around a core of gunpowder. He had sacrificed a fair amount of spare ammunition to provide the powder, but each bundle was a potential fire bomb, fused with sun-dried buffalo grass and ready to flare up at the touch of a match. Gunn tied several bundles to the tails of the hobbled ponies, then cut the others free. Trained to wait, the animals remained within the confines of the herd while he grouped the still-hobbled beasts at the farther edge of the area. Then he slashed the confining thongs and lit the fire bombs.

The mustangs twisted, wickering as the fuses burned down. Then the powder ignited and balls of bright flame erupted around their haunches. They screamed and stampeded, taking the others with them in a maddened rush that charged straight through the camp.

The Comanches came instantly awake as the ponies hit. They had split into tribal groups, and the herd Gunn had spooked contained about forty animals. Their fright communicated to the other herds and the mustangs tried to join the stampede. Suddenly the night was filled with the terrified screams of the mustangs and the shouts of confused Indians. Gunn added to the chaos by hurling more fire bombs at random into the camp. Then he turned and ran for his own horse.

A second guard moved to cut him off. Gunn hit the Comanche on the run, cannoning into the smaller man so that he crashed back, falling down. Without breaking stride, Gunn drew his Colt, firing directly into the man's face. Then he was past the body, heading for the buffalo wallow.

He swung into the saddle and lifted the roan out of the depression. Three more Comanches ran towards him and he emptied the Colt in their direction. One collapsed with a hole in his ribs, the others turned back, looking for their ponies, and Gunn was gone into the night. He rode hard, knowing that pursuit would soon follow, seeking to build a head start, enough to lead the Indians away from the ranch.

The defenders of the Flying D listened in bewilderment to the noise outside. They could hear the Indian ponies screaming in terror, the clamour of the braves. Fire showed yellow against the darkness, seeming to race over the desert in wild patterns. But there was no way they could understand what was going on. Had they known, they might have tried to make a break then. Instead, they waited for daylight.

Iron Knife waited for nothing. He grabbed the mane of a galloping pony and swung astride the animal, shouting for his people to follow him. Then, backed by a handful of warriors, he turned the stampeding mustangs in a wide circle, driving them back towards the Indians waiting on foot. A few ponies ran free, but most of the herd was turned and recaptured. It took some time and it gave Gunn the start he needed.

Dawn lit the Staked Plains with pale, grey light. It showed a lone figure riding at an easy canter towards the south. Behind him came a group of thirty men, their faces angry beneath their war paint, their ponies running hard to gain ground on the fugitive.

Gunn watched them closing up and heeled the big roan to a faster pace. The gelding responded with a burst of speed that put distance on the Comanches. He used it to find cover.

A wash showed ahead and he went down the bank at full gallop, turned the roan eastwards and followed the dried-out stream bed until he spotted a south-pointing feeder creek. He kept going until cactus blocked his path, then took the horse up the bank onto the plain. The Comanches had followed him into the wash and were now invisible. Gunn urged the roan back to full gallop, looking for more cover.

He was confident of losing his pursuers, but disappointed that only part of the war band had come after him. The Comanches were far better disciplined than usual, and he wondered who wore the feathers of paramount war chief that he could hold the fractious Nemmenna in such tight check.

Iron Knife had exerted all his authority to prevent his entire war party from taking off after the mysterious rider.

The two braves who had spotted the man had not recognised him. All they could tell the war chief was that he was very fast and very good with a gun; he looked like a white man, but moved like an Indian. That he had managed to come amongst them unnoticed and stampede the horse herd was, of itself, evidence of Indian-like skill. That he was now escaping was a vicious blow to Iron Knife's pride. Snarling his displeasure, the war chief called Little Buffalo to him, organising a pursuit. Then he set to calming his disturbed followers in readiness for the morning's attack.

When the sun rose, he was in a savage humour. With thirty warriors committed to the chase, and half that number killed in the fighting, his original band was cut down to few more than fifty braves. And the ranch still stood.

Iron Knife stared towards the hated building, trying to devise some means of getting inside.

Matthew Gunn kept running. He had a half-mile lead on the Comanches and the cross-bred gelding was holding its own. He didn't know how long the Indians would keep after him before deciding they'd come far enough and turning back to the ranch, but at least he had pulled some out of the fight. Enough to give the people inside a better chance.

He rounded a mesa and grinned as luck placed a friendly hand on his shoulder.

Up ahead a column of men was riding towards him. They were dressed in beat-up American clothes, each man armed with a carbine and at least one pistol. Their mounts were big, reliable-looking horses, covering ground at an easy, loping pace. As he came closer, he could see the six-pointed stars pinned to jackets and shirts: the badge of the Texas Rangers.

They saw him coming and he hollered, pointing back at the Indians.

The Rangers looked towards the mesa, saw the Comanches, and charged. The Indians spotted them seconds later and began to whoop, dashing their ponies head-on at the column. They outnumbered the Texans thirty to twenty, and they anticipated an easy victory.

Gunn turned his own horse as the Rangers came level, heading back the way he had come with his Winchester held in both hands.

'Name's Abrams,' bellowed the leading Ranger. 'Captain Abrams.'

'Pleased to know you,' Gunn shouted back.

'Yeah,' Abrams yelled. 'Looks like you could use some company.'

The two groups hit at full gallop. Three Rangers went down with bullets staining blood across their shirt-fronts, but more Comanches fell to the disciplined fire of the volunteer lawmen. Abrams took his men past the Indians, then spun his horse in its own length and charged back. The Rangers fired on the run, then used their heavier mounts to batter down the Comanche ponies. After the second charge only half the Indians were still alive. They whooped and came in again, and this time Abrams called his men to stand. They sat their horses and picked off the painted warriors like marksmen at a turkey shoot. Three Comanches toppled to the sand and the remainder broke and ran, heading back towards the mesa.

Abrams shouted for his Rangers to let them go and turned to Gunn.

'Where you from, mister?' He was pushing cartridges into his Winchester as he spoke.

'Came from the Flying D,' answered Gunn, 'they got a whole lot of trouble there.'

'That so?' Abrams slid the Winchester into the saddle boot. 'Figgered they might. We're headin' that way.'

'Mind if I ride along?' Gunn asked.

Abrams shook his head, studying Gunn's face.

'I seen you anyplace before?' He asked. 'Seems to me I know you.'

Gunn recalled the bounty posted on him for killing the Ranger sergeant and shook his head, hoping Abrams was too busy chasing hostiles to start thinking about reward notices.

'Don't think so,' he said evenly, 'I rode in from California.'

'Shoulda stayed there,' grunted Abrams. 'It's quieter.'

He called his men into line and they set out for the Flying D.

Nolan watched the activity in front of the ranch. Something had spooked the Indians during the night and he estimated their numbers to be lower than the day before. But now something was going on and it made him tetchy that he didn't know what it was.

He found out soon enough.

A wagon appeared through the dust, pushed by several braves. It was piled high with buffalo grass and timber from the burned-out wreckage of the bunkhouse and the barn. The high tailgate and the weathered plank sides protected the Comanches from his gun, and he began to swear softly as he realised what they were planning.

He shouted for Christie to use the Sharps on the wagon, but not even the big buffalo gun could penetrate the woodwork, at least not until it got too close for comfort. By then the Indians were too eager to close in to take much notice of the bullets. Nolan tried firing under the wagon, and succeeded in crippling three Comanches. Christie got two more by shooting straight through the rig as it came up to the main door. But then it hit the oak panelling and horsemen charged in from either side, ignoring the fusillade that echoed around them as they lifted the pushers in flying pick-ups and headed back out of range.

Then the fire arrows started again.

Three landed dead centre of the piled grass and the wagon began to burn. It caught slowly at first, the grass crackling as rivulets of flame darted swiftly through the sun-bleached stems. Then the charred timbers caught, adding a steady swirl of flame that ignited the bodywork of the wagon itself. Smoke, black and stinking, began to pour in around the edges of the door, and the metal rivets grew hot. Nolan shouted for water and blankets, and Dalton called two cowhands from the windows to sluice the door and hang a blanket over the timber. They soaked the cloth, which helped stem the smoke, but they knew it was only a matter of time before the door itself caught fire.

And then the way would be open for the Comanches.

The Indians continued to press the attack against all four sides, risking more casualties as they drew men from the fire-fighting to man the gun ports. They lost warriors, but they bought the time it took for the main door to catch fire.

Christie threw water over the blanket, but it dried quickly, and as he used his carbine, the material began to smoulder. Soon, the lower edge grew black, then red, then tongues of flame swept up the blanket. It was ignored as the Comanches pressed home a new assault.

Abruptly, a gush of heat spat across the room and a long, flickering jet of flame burst from the door. The wood crackled, blackening. Then the central portion collapsed inwards, clouding the room with sparks and smoke.

Anxious to count first coup, a young brave hurled himself through the flames. Nolan shot him as he landed inside, then fired the Winchester from the hip, straight through the door.

For the moment, the Comanches fell back, but fire crept over the floor, and the two men knew that in minutes the room would be an inferno.

Still shooting, they drew back to the side rooms as the Comanches came in.

CHAPTER NINE

Captain Abrams halted his Rangers a half mile out from the Flying D.

The ranch house was burning and around the main door the Comanches were clustered thicker than flies on new-fallen horse apples. Abrams watched them, his lips moving as he tried to count.

'Hell,' he grunted, turning to Gunn, 'I ain't never seen so many injuns out here. Wonder what riled 'em up.'

'Comancheros,' murmured the blond man, checking his weapons. 'They been supplying guns.'

'You can tell me about it later,' said Abrams. 'You want in on this? Or you chicken?'

'It's a free range,' said Gunn coldly, 'an' I got a personal interest.'

'Good.' Abrams smoothed back his thinning hair and glanced round at his men. They were waiting for his word to go. 'When I holler, you stick with me; I don't aim to holler twice.'

He waved his arm and the Rangers moved their horses to line abreast. The arm fell and the line began to walk forwards. The pace increased to a trot that got steadily faster, rising to a canter. A quarter mile from the ranch the Rangers were covering ground fast and the Indians still hadn't seen them. Then Abrams yelled and the line plunged forwards, boots and spurs accelerating the horses to a headlong gallop.

The Comanches spotted the attack too late. By the time they turned to meet the Rangers, the Texans were in amongst them, killing with a ferocity that matched the Indians own savagery.

Gunn emptied his Winchester and drew his Colt. When that was emptied, he used his knife, slashing and stabbing a path to the door. The Rangers were badly outnumbered, but the sheer violence of their attack drove the Comanches back. More accustomed to freewheeling horseback fights than this kind of close-range battle, the Indians were at a disadvantage. Their confusion was increased by the counter-attack from inside the ranch.

Led by Nolan and Christie, Dalton and his men came out fighting.

Ten Indians were bottled up in the main room. They went down under the concentrated fire of the survivors. Then the defenders came out into the open to back the Rangers.

Iron Knife saw his men going down and screamed for a retreat. He turned his own pony and ran for the open plain. Behind him, the Comanches broke off the struggle and fled. They had lost thirty warriors.

The Rangers let them go. What no-one knew was that four warriors were still inside the ranch. They had scaled the walls during the confusion of the Ranger attack, dropping into the courtyard where they killed two cowboys, and moving through the house. They heard Iron Knife's shouted order to retreat and went back the way they had come in.

On the way, they spotted Eleanor Dalton.

The woman screamed when she saw the Indians, but her cry was drowned by gunfire. She lifted the rifle she was holding, but the leading Comanche knocked it aside, then swung his war club back against Eleanor's temple. She collapsed without a sound. The Indians picked her up, climbed to the roof, and rode away. Eleanor Dalton was draped over the shoulders of the leading pony.

Iron Knife reached the main camp without further incident. He was in an ugly mood and the news of successful attacks in other parts of the territory served only to heighten his anger at his own failure.

Samuel Graves and John Bear were still tied to the stakes,

though now in considerably worse condition. Beard stubble covered their filthy cheeks and their clothes were smeared with spilled food and blood. The Indian women had fed them – as casually as they fed their dogs – and amused themselves tormenting the two men. When the squaws weren't hurting them, the children used them as targets for their practice arrows. Their bodies were cramped by the confinement, and because no-one had thought to loose them, the stink of ordure vied with the reek of their sweat.

Iron Knife smiled when he saw them. Their degradation cheered him a little.

'Moon soon get thin,' he said, poking Graves with his Winchester. 'You think old one come back?'

He laughed and walked away.

Abrams' Rangers helped douse the fires threatening to finish the Comanches' work. Four of Dalton's hired hands were dead, and three more wounded. The rancher himself wore a ragged bandage around his head, blood from a hatchet wound seeping through the smoke-grimed cloth.

Nolan and Christie were unharmed and the first thing they did when the fighting ceased was help themselves to Dalton's whisky. The rancher made no move to stop them, and after a moment's thought, passed bottles out to his men and the Rangers. The two scalphunters carried theirs through to the courtyard, where the air was cleaner. So they didn't see Matthew Gunn enter the ranch house.

Gunn turned down Dalton's offer of a drink. He studied the men around him, looking for Nolan and Christie. When he couldn't find them, he asked Dalton.

'Why sure,' said the rancher, 'they're around someplace. They done real well in the fight.'

'Yeah,' grunted Gunn. 'They like killing Indians.'

Dalton looked at him curiously. 'They friends o' yours?'

'Not exactly.' Gunn's voice was low, cold. 'They met my folks.'

'Try the yard,' Dalton suggested, 'I gotta go see Eleanor.'

Gunn went through to the courtyard. A handful of Rangers were cleaning up around the spring and he ignored them. On the far side of the area he could see Nolan talking with Christie. They hadn't seen him, and he drew his Colt, thumbing back the hammer as he started across the courtyard.

Then a hand grasped his wrist and a pistol barrel dug into his ribs.

'Let's you an' me have that talk,' said Abrams quietly.

He steered Gunn off to the side into a bedroom, and kicked the door shut.

'Somethin's troublin' you, mister. You wanta tell me about it?'

Gunn shook his head. 'It's personal.'

'Friend,' Abrams said evenly, 'right now we're in the middle of an injun war. You mentioned Comancheros earlier. That makes it my business.' His voice grew harsh. 'Why was you fixin' to gun them two?'

The blond man watched the Ranger's face for a moment, thinking. He didn't know where Abrams stood on the question of scalp hunting. It could be that the Ranger captain would side with Nolan and Christie; or he might come down the other way. Whatever, there wasn't too much choice: Abrams was holding a levelled gun and he wanted answers.

'They killed my parents. They ran a scalp hunting outfit that hit my folks' place. I been chasing them since.'

'How come they took white hair?' Abrams sounded sceptical.

Gunn shrugged. 'My mother was Chiricahua Apache.'

'Hey!' Abrams was abruptly alert. 'So you're a 'breed. What you call yoreself?'

'Gunn,' he answered. 'Matthew Gunn.'

Abrams scratched his head. 'Also known as Azul. And wanted fer killin' a Ranger sergeant.'

'He drew first. It was self-defence.'

'That's as maybe.' Abrams friendly attitude was gone now. 'But he was still a Ranger.'

'So what're you planning to do?' Gunn asked, easing his hand slowly towards his Colt. 'Kill me on the spot? Or do I get a trial?'

'That's kinda difficult,' admitted Abrams. 'You're one problem I coulda done without right now. How's about givin' me that pistol fer starters. With yore left hand.'

Gunn reached across to the Colt and handed it to the Ranger.

'Now we'll check things out with them two,' murmured Abrams.

Still holding his revolver on Gunn's belly, he opened the door and called one of his men over. A few seconds later Nolan and Christie entered the room with two Rangers close behind.

'Sweet Jesus!' Christie started to draw as he spoke. 'It's him!'

Nolan said nothing. Just stood with his cold, green eyes fixed on Gunn.

'Hold it, mister.' Abrams' voice was a whiplash sound in the tensed room, and a Ranger grabbed Christie's gunhand, shoving the Colt down in the holster.

'We got kinda different views on a story,' Abrams continued. 'This feller claims you two scalped his folks. That right?'

Christie started to say something, but Nolan glanced at him and the Southerner clammed up.

'We tangled with some Chiricahuas one time,' Nolan said, 'an' he's been followin' us since. Could be his folks was part o' the bunch. Fact is, he ain't nothin' but a 'breed. An' he's wanted.'

He paused, grinning at Gunn.

'You check yore dodgers, Captain. You'll find he's wanted on both sides o' the border. Killed a man in Mexico an' then a Ranger in Piedras Negras. He killed friends o' mine, too.'

'Yeah.' Christie joined in. 'Luis an' Manolo was real close. He killed 'em both.'

'What about Carson City?' Gunn asked quietly. 'Remember that?'

'What about it?' Abrams turned to him, curious.

'They hit the bank,' said Gunn. 'Killed everyone inside an' headed for the hills. They found a wagon train on the way. Stole the horses.'

'Now that,' said Abrams sharply, 'is one helluva accusation.'

'Check with Carson City or Stockton.' Gunn pressed his point. 'The law there'll confirm it.'

'That,' remarked Abrams sarcastically, 'might be kinda difficult right now. The real fact o' the matter appears to be that you're wanted in Texas. Could well be yore story's true, an' these fellers are on the dodge from the law same as you. Trouble is there ain't no way I can check that.'

'Give me back my gun,' said the halfbreed, 'and leave us alone. We can sort it out ourselves.'

'Anytime,' Nolan snarled.

'That's one solution,' nodded Abrams, 'but it ain't exactly a legal-type answer. You fellers just sit a spell while I figger out what to do about you.'

He thought for a while, staring at nothing. After a while he nodded to himself and spoke again.

'I guess I'm duty-bound to bring you in,' he pointed at Gunn. 'I'm kinda sorry about it: you helped us a considerable amount. But there ain't no two ways to it. I gotta take you back.'

Christie laughed out loud and Nolan grinned. Then they both stopped as Abrams turned to face them.

'An' you two better come along as well. If what Gunn here says is right, you'll be posted. There ain't enough of us to go chasin' them Comanch', so we'll all ride over to Abilene.'

He motioned to the Rangers standing behind Nolan and Christie, and the Texans lifted their guns.

'Alright,' smiled Abrams. 'Now let's go.'

He turned towards the door, gesturing for the prisoners to go through first. Then stopped as a hoarse despairing cry echoed through the wreckage of the Flying D.

'Eleanor!' It was Dalton's voice. 'They took Eleanor.'

Abrams went through the door fast. Dalton saw him and hooked desperate hands into the Ranger's shirt.

'My wife! The injuns got my wife!'

'Oh, fuck!' Abrams snarled. 'If I ain't got enough problems already.'

He sighed, lifting Dalton's clutching fingers away from his shirt.

'How'd you know, Nat?'

'She's gone! She was with us through the fight but now she's gone.'

'Dammit!' Grunted Abrams. 'They must've took her when they got inside. Alright, Nat. Calm down. We'll go after her.'

He turned away, talking mostly to himself.

'They probably ain't killed her yet.'

'Can you get her back?' Dalton's voice was on the verge of cracking.

'Don't rightly know,' said Abrams slowly. 'Way them injuns was runnin' they must have taken her along to their camp. Trouble is, we don't know where they're located.'

'I do,' said Gunn clearly.

'Mister, you better not be tryin' anything.' Abrams' eyes bored into Gunn's.

'I'm not,' replied Gunn evenly. 'I spotted the camp riding out here. I can take you to it.'

'Friend,' grinned Abrams, 'you got yoreself a job. Spot us that camp an' I'll listen to yore story over again.'

'It's a deal,' said Gunn.

CHAPTER TEN

The Comanches raped Eleanor Dalton when they got back to the main camp. To her surprise, they left her alone during the journey, treating her roughly, but not touching her except when it was necessary. She had fully expected them to throw her down on the sand as soon as they were clear of pursuit, and in some ways this unexpected twist unnerved her more than would the act itself.

But Iron Knife changed the situation.

The war chief was still smarting from his defeat and the woman represented a chance to repay the whites. When his braves threw her before him, he ripped her torn dress away and took her in full view of his people. A woman less resilient than Eleanor might have lost her mind, but the years of living lonely on the Staked Plains had imbued her with that degree of toughness that marked Frontier wives. Groaning beneath the Comanche's muscular body, she resigned herself to the inevitable. It wasn't enjoyable, but at least she was still alive.

When Iron Knife had spent himself, he called for both his wives and ordered them to bathe the white woman and dress her in clothes befitting a Comanche squaw.

Eleanor Dalton was attractive, and still young enough to bear children. In time Iron Knife would sell her, if not to one of his own warriors, then to the Kiowas or maybe the Mexicans. Either way, she represented wealth and the sweet taste of vengeance.

Samuel Graves watched the performance and guessed what was on Iron Knife's mind. It gave him an idea that might – just – win him a chance to get free.

He was brooding on it when scouts brought word of the search party headed for the camp.

Gunn had serious doubts about the chances of the searchers. One or two men, skilled in the art of Indian fighting, might get close enough to the Comanches to bring the woman out. Abrams' group was too large to hide, too small to stand a chance in open fight. There were seventeen Texas Rangers, Abrams himself, Nolan, Christie and Dalton. It was too many.

Abrams, though, refused to divide his men. Until the Comanches showed.

They appeared out of nowhere, riding silently on either side of the whites.

Gunn turned to Abrams as the Indians drew closer.

'Like I said: we're too easy to find.'

'Looks like you was right, too,' grunted the Ranger reluctantly. 'Got any suggestions now?'

'Yeah.' Gunn glanced to either side. 'When I give the word, tell your men to start running. There's a mesa a half-day's ride from here. The Comancheros hid a shipment of guns there. If we can reach it, we can hold them off.'

'What about Mizz Dalton?'

Gunn shrugged. 'I told you it was a job for one man. I'll break away and find her.'

'Call it a job fer two,' Abrams replied, 'I'm comin' with you.'

'Make that three.' Dalton had overheard them.

Gunn shook his head. 'Not him. He sees his wife an' gets excited, he could spoil the whole thing.'

'Sorry, Nat.' Abrams placed a sympathetic hand on Dalton's shoulder. 'But he's right. We'll get her back for you.'

He let his horse fall back down the line, whispering instructions to the others. Then he fell into step alongside Gunn, waiting for the halfbreed's signal.

Gunn watched the Comanches. They were toying with the whites, playing a game of nerves before attacking. He waited, gauging the moment, then he shouted and heeled the roan into a spurt.

The move took the Comanches by surprise, giving the column a fragile chance. Before the Indians could reach full gallop, the whites were out in front, riding hell for leather southwards. The Comanches held the advantage of numbers, but the Rangers were used to fighting off horseback, and their fire was more accurate, downing several Indians in the first moments of the running fight. Then it turned into a straight chase as the Rangers, unpleasantly aware of their depleted supply of ammunition concentrated on staying ahead. They hit a wash at full gallop and Gunn shouted to Abrams, turning his horse.

The Ranger Captain lunged alongside and they thundered down the wash as the main body went up the far bank. The stream bed turned after a few yards and they were hidden from view as the Comanches poured whooping over the rim.

They waited until the sounds of battle faded into the afternoon, then turned northwards, heading for the Comanche village.

They rode nervously, watching the desert, but no more Indians showed. They kept going until the waning moon was directly overhead and Gunn called a halt: their horses needed the rest. It was a cold camp, and what little food they had brought with them was eaten in silence before Abrams settled down to sleep and Gunn stood watch.

He woke the Ranger after a couple of hours and prepared to grab some sleep himself. Abrams grinned as he settled down to watch, looking curiously at his companion.

'You're a strange kind o' feller, ain't you? You could've gotten away. How come you stayed?'

'I gave you my word,' replied the halfbreed quietly.

'I still aim to take you in,' murmured Abrams. 'You thought about that?'

'Sure,' grinned Gunn, 'but right now tomorrow's enough to think about.'

'Yeah.' Abrams sounded thoughtful. 'Was the shootin' like you said?'

'Which one?' Gunn asked. 'There's been quite a few.'

'Piedras,' Abrams explained, 'the Ranger.'

'I killed a Ranger, sure,' Gunn murmured. 'But it was him or me. Nolan set me up. He spun the Ranger a yarn.'

'Well,' said Abrams slowly, 'I guess we'll hafta question Nolan back in Abilene.'

'If we ever get there,' said Gunn softly.

Then he settled down to sleep.

The Rangers lost four men before they reached the mesa, and their ammunition was nearly spent. They recognised the place from Gunn's description and hit the slope at full gallop. The rock was no more than twenty feet off the plain and on top there was barely sufficient room for all the horses. But it gave them the advantage they needed. And when they uncovered the cache, they knew they were halfway safe.

Gleefully, they discarded their old weapons, choosing brand-new Winchesters from Graves' stock which they put to immediate use.

The mesa afforded a clear field of fire, and the few Comanches brave – or foolish – enough to attempt the incline were shot from their ponies before they even got close. Soon a litter of corpses, human and animal, blockaded the slope, and the Rangers settled down to picking off the warriors sniping at them from the flatlands.

After a while the Indians gave up and drew back out of range. They kept up a sporadic fire, enough to hold the Texans on the mesa, and the defenders waited. Their plan was to pull out under cover of darkness, so they tried to rest, preparing for the escape.

Nathaniel Dalton offered to stand the middle watch and the sergeant in command tied Nolan and Christie by wrists and ankles before rolling himself in his blanket and falling immediately asleep.

It was full dark when Nolan came to. Something had woke him, and when he opened his eyes he saw Dalton cutting through his bonds.

The rancher motioned for him to keep quiet and finished cutting. Then he freed Christie and beckoned the two men to follow him. They moved silently to the rim of the mesa, and saw that Dalton had wrapped strips of blanket over the hooves of three horses.

'Lissen,' whispered the rancher, 'I got three thousand gold eagles stashed back at the Flying D. It's all yours if you'll help me get Eleanor back.'

'What about Abrams and the 'breed?' Nolan put his mouth close to Dalton's ear.

'Dammit! She's my wife,' came the answer.

'Yeah.' In the dark Dalton couldn't see Nolan's smile. 'That she is.'

'You want it, or not?' Dalton asked.

'Let's go,' replied the dark man.

They led their horses off the mesa and walked them westwards. When Nolan decided they were far enough out, they mounted and rode quietly away. They described a long half circle before he felt it safe enough to turn back, north and east, heading for where he thought the Indian village was located.

The Rangers woke at dawn and found them gone. There was nothing they could do about it because the Comanches were pressing a renewed attack and all their time was taken up staying alive.

Dalton's betrayal meant that their escape plan was useless and they had to sit out another day under the sun. When night fell, they prepared to leave. Two more men were dead, and three badly hurt. They all promised themselves a fast revenge if they ever encountered Dalton or the two hardcases again.

Most of them got safely away from the mesa, but when the

Comanches picked up their trail the next morning two of the wounded were killed in the fighting and more hurt.

Of the original company of twenty men, only nine made it back to Abilene.

From the Red River south to Austin, and west from Fort Worth to the Pecos, Texas was in an uproar. The Comanches, and to a lesser extent the Kiowas, had always been a problem. Now they were a savage threat to the whole territory. Suddenly, the horse warriors were hitting all over the Lone Star State. Cavalry patrols out of Forts Worth, Concho, Davis and Stockton did what they could to stem the flood of war. Fort Quitman had its hands full with the Apaches, probing southwards as the thin-spread forces of yellow legs were pulled away from the New Mexican border to handle Comanches.

It was a desperate struggle, and more often than not, the cavalry arrived on the scene of a fight too late to do anything for the slaughtered whites.

The Army fought by a book the Indians had never read. Faced with a roving patrol, the Comanches attacked when they were strong enough, ran when they were outnumbered. The cavalry expected a formal order of battle, not the hit-and-run skirmishes favoured by their painted opponents, and they ended up chasing will o' the wisp riders who came and killed and went with savage enthusiasm.

It fell to the Texas Rangers to hit the Indians with their own tactics. And the Rangers were even thinner on the ground than the Army.

Texas looked set for a full-scale Indian war.

Matthew Gunn crawled silently down the slope to where Abrams waited beside the muzzled horses. He motioned for the Ranger to follow him, and they pulled back away from the Comanche village.

They found cover in a bluff about a mile from the camp.

A cleft split the rock wide enough to take both horses, and they herded the animals in, settling down to plan their next move.

'I think I can get into the camp.' Gunn scraped a fire together as he spoke. 'We'll wait until night, then I'll go in.'

'They'll spot you sure.' Abrams pointed at the mane of pale hair. 'That'll give you away.'

Gunn smiled and shook his head. 'Not when I've finished.'

He slipped out of the cleft and scaled the bluff. Beyond the rim he found the plants he was looking for, and began to collect berries and leaves. He filled his hat and returned to the hide-out, where Abrams had the fire going. It was made of dry wood and gave off hardly any smoke, the faint whisps that did rise dissipating against the rock face before reaching the clear air above.

Gunn used a stone to crush the plants he had gathered, pouring the sticky pulp into a billycan provided by Abrams. Then he set the can over the fire and began to stir the mixture. He added a little water and watched the brew turn slowly to a thick, black liquid. Carefully, he lifted the can and set it aside to cool. After a while he tested the stuff with a finger, nodding at the result.

'What in the hell is it?' Abrams was curious and impatient.

'Wait,' murmured Gunn, 'you'll find out soon enough.'

He stripped off his shirt and bent over the billycan. Delicately, he began to smear the liquid over his hair. The blond mane turned gradually darker until it was completely black.

'Hey,' Abrams whistled softly, surprised, 'now I would figger you for an Apache.'

'Or a Comanche,' Gunn grinned. 'It's a good dye.'

He smeared more of the stuff over his face, painting bands across his forehead and nose. He blackened one cheek and used the remainder to paint broad stripes across his chest.

Then he stood up. 'How do I look?'

'Like a Comanche,' grunted Abrams, 'you better hope none o' my Rangers hit the camp when you're in there.'

'You better hope it doesn't rain,' said Gunn. 'This should fool them at night, but if it washes off I'm about . . .'

'Cleaned up,' Abrams finished. 'I hope not.'

'Yeah, so do I.'

He let the dye dry out through what remained of the afternoon, and then, as dusk turned into night, he set off on foot. He was wrapped in a patterned blanket and carried his Winchester and the two knives. The Colt he left with Abrams: if he was spotted none of the weapons would be much use.

The Comanche village was noisy, the braves celebrating their victories around the fires. They were too confident of their strength to post nightguards, and Gunn slipped easily through the outer rings of lodges. He walked casually, though his nerves were fine-honed, his trigger finger ready to squeeze off a shot if necessary. It was not: the Indians were too intent on recounting their various battles, displaying the scalps they had taken, to question one more warrior strolling through the village. He got close to the central area and paused, watching from the shadows. The scaffolds he had seen before were gone, but the two men he had noticed remained, and he was surprised when he saw that one was black. He realised that they must be the surviving Comancheros, and smiled: they had got what they deserved.

On the far side of the open space was a lodge larger than the others. It was decorated with symbols of the hunt and of war, and two coup sticks were planted to either side of the entrance flap. They both carried an array of scalps.

Then the flap lifted and a Comanche woman came out. There was a scuffle, and a second woman was propelled violently into the open.

Gunn recognised Eleanor Dalton from her husband's description.

Eleanor was confused. The fear she had known during her first hours in the Comanche village was gone now, replaced by nervous wondering and the beginnings of anger. It was obvious that the Indians did not plan to kill her, nor had the men approached her. The squaws, though rough, had done nothing more than dress her in greasy doeskins and set her to work.

The two men staked out in the middle of the camp suffered far worse.

Even though her first thoughts were purely for herself, Eleanor couldn't help wondering about the other prisoners. The negro had followed her with his eyes when she walked through the camp, jerking his head whenever he saw her looking in a way that made it obvious he wanted to talk. But the Comanche women had given her no opportunity. The black man and his halfbreed companion were ignored by all, except the women who fed them and the children who used them as targets.

Eleanor was too concerned with her own safety to worry about them, but freed, they might help her escape. The trouble was, she couldn't get near them.

Now she let the chief's women drive her over to the cooking fires. They jabbered at her in their outlandish tongue, gesturing at the pots until she realised that she was meant to carry food to the warriors.

Iron Knife wanted to show off his captive.

Nathaniel Dalton forced himself to curb the impatience that gritted his teeth with impotent fury. Frontier sense told him that Nolan was doing the right thing swinging a circle round the Comanches, approaching slowly; but worry about his wife prompted him to go in blind. He tried arguing it with the dark man, but the cold eyes and the biting voice shut him up. He hated to admit it, but Nolan scared him. Christie wasn't much better, not with that hysterical laugh and obvious delight in killing. But it was Nolan's implacable calm that really worried him. It was as though the man knew something Dalton didn't, and was hoarding the secret, gloating silently over the knowledge. It fretted Dalton.

A while later he got really scared.

Nolan reined in, calling a rest stop, and turned casually to the rancher.

'Where'd you say you hid those eagles?' A faint hint of a smile showed on his mouth.

'I didn't,' muttered Dalton. 'I'll pay after we get Eleanor back.'

'Could be you won't make it,' said Nolan, his voice conversational.

'Then Eleanor can show you.'

'Suppose she don't make it?'

'You're out o' luck.' Dalton wondered if he could beat Nolan to the draw. He knew he couldn't.

'No.' The conversational tone went as fast as it had come. 'Not us. You.'

'What the hell you mean?' Dalton could feel sweat on his spine. It wasn't from the sun.

'We take on a job o' work,' rasped Nolan, 'we expect to get paid for it.'

'I'll pay you. I promise.' Dalton tried to buy time.

'A dead man can't pay no-one.' The voice was harsh, as menacing as the Colt that seemed to jump into Nolan's fist.

'What the hell!' Dalton spluttered. 'What's yore game?'

'No game friend,' murmured Nolan. 'I'm playin' fer keeps.'

Dalton stared at the gun. Behind him, he heard the hammer of Christie's Colt click back. It sounded very loud.

'I'll count to three,' Nolan grinned. 'Then I'm gonna shoot you. The first one'll bust yore knee. Then yore elbow. The third'll put a hole through yore gut.'

'No!' Dalton squealed.

'One.'

'Get Eleanor first.'

'Two.'

'I'll pay you then, I swear.'

'Three.'

'I'll tell you! Oh, dear God. I'll tell you.'

'Thought you might.' Nolan kept his gun levelled on the rancher.

Dalton swallowed hard, conscious of a wetness spreading down his legs.

'The fountain in the courtyard.' He shifted in his saddle, trying to ease the uncomfortable dampness in his pants. 'There is a loose stone on the north wall. The money's under it.'

'Thanks, Dalton.' Nolan smiled. 'You're real obliging.'

Then he fired. Twice.

The first bullet smashed through Dalton's chest, slamming him backwards in his saddle. His eyes opened very wide and he began to say something, but the blood pumping from his ruptured lung clogged his throat and he could only groan. The second shot hit him under the chin, smashing his jaw before it drove on into his brain. The rancher toppled back, slipping to one side as his left foot came out of the stirrup. His horse, already nervous, spooked as the body slid down its haunches. It jerked away from the touch of the dead flesh, felt the weight gone from its back, and took off across the desert.

It ran blind, trying to escape the thing that bumped behind it. But Dalton's right boot was hooked firmly through the stirrup and the animal succeeded only in dragging the corpse.

After a while, Dalton was no longer recognisable.

Christie giggled as he watched the big horse run, and turned to Nolan.

'Where now? You figger to get the woman?'

Nolan looked at the Southerner and spat.

'You crazy, Jude?' His voice was flat. 'If she's still alive, she's either mad or in some buck's bed. I ain't got no more use for her.'

They turned their horses and began to ride in the direction of the Flying D.

CHAPTER ELEVEN

Samuel Graves looked up at the sky and mouthed an obscenity. Night was a blue velvet cloth pricked through by the white silver points of the stars. The moon was a pale yellow sliver; and there was no sign of Paco.

The negro was suddenly aware of a low-pitched humming sound from close by his right shoulder, and he turned to John Bear. The halfbreed was sitting with his eyes tight shut and his mouth open, chanting softly. Graves recognised the chant: it was a death song. He cursed some more and tried to dream up a convincing argument for staying alive. But he couldn't think of anything that would persuade Iron Knife, so he concentrated instead on trying to make himself comfortable. It was impossible.

He watched the Comanche chieftains seated around the main fire, taking food from the women, grinning and shouting as the new white prisoner moved amongst them.

Then his gut knotted painfully as Iron Knife stood up, shouting and pointing at the two men.

He couldn't hear what the war chief was saying through the babble of voices, but the intention was clear as the Comanche strode, smiling, towards his prisoners. He stopped before the stakes, watching Graves' face with studied calm. Then he squatted and reached out, clamping steel-hard fingers over the negro's jaw so that Graves was forced to look directly at him.

'The moon is thin.' His voice was soft, full of menace. 'And the old one has not returned with the guns. It is time for you to die, black one.'

Graves tried to say something, but Iron Knife's fingers constricted his mouth so that only an incoherent moaning came out.

'It will be very slow,' continued the Comanche, 'and very painful. And you will know what is going to happen because we shall kill the other one first.'

John Bear opened his eyes and looked over at Iron Knife. His lip curled and hate shone from his face.

'The Comanches are women. They talk like women and their strength is a woman's. My father was Kiowa. I am not afraid of the Comanche squaw-warriors.'

It was the first time he had spoken since being tied, and the longest speech Graves had ever heard him give. It ended abruptly when Iron Knife kicked him in the stomach.

They cut John Bear free and dragged him over to the centre of the camp. Stakes were already hammered into the packed sand and they threw the halfbreed down, lashing his wrists and ankes to the posts, so that he was spreadeagled in full view of the Indians. Iron Knife hunkered down beside him, grinning as he cut John Bear's clothing from his body.

'So the Nemmenna are women? We shall see what the white Kiowa thinks of our women.'

He called out to the squaws serving the food, and they giggled, setting down the serving dishes and hurrying over to the sprawled figure. Iron Knife spoke with them a moment, then resumed his position on the chief's blanket.

Chuckling and crooning, the women set to work.

Matthew Gunn watched from the shadows. He felt no pity for the Comancheros: they dealt in death, and a painful end was one of the risks they took in return for selling weapons at inflated prices. The diversion caused by their suffering could, though, be useful to him if it provided a means of getting close to the Dalton woman.

For the moment she was too close to the chiefs, standing in horrified silence as she watched the squaws working on the prisoner.

The man held out for a long time before he began to scream and Eleanor Dalton doubled over, vomiting.

Gunn saw the Comanche chief lean aside and grasp the woman by her wrist, pulling her down as he spoke. He used English, and Gunn could just make out the words.

'Watch carefully. You learn. You work on *El Negro*.'

Graves choked on the fear clogging his throat, wishing he could tear his eyes away from John Bear's ravaged body. It was impossible: the awful sight was as compelling as it was horrifying. He had always known that the Comanches were cruel, but until now it had been the kind of knowledge that is registered and then pushed deliberately to the back of the mind, a reference that concerns other people. Now the terrifying reality was stretched bloodily before him. He hoped that John Bear would take a long time to die, staving off his own fate. Maybe Iron Knife would change his mind. Maybe a cavalry patrol would jump the camp. Maybe Paco would turn up.

Maybe it would snow in mid-summer.

Graves shuddered and listened to the halfbreed screaming.

The noise went on for a long time. Shrill at first, it grew hoarse as the night grew older, dropping to a guttural, choking moan that in turn fell to a breathy whimper.

When it stopped altogether, the silence was very loud.

Iron Knife rose to his feet, dragging Eleanor Dalton with him. He handed her to a squaw, then waited as two braves dragged Graves across the clearing.

The negro was stiff from his long confinement, his arms and legs cramping badly when he tried to stand. The Comanches held him upright, bracing him when he flexed away from the blade in Iron Knife's hand. The war chief smiled and slashed through Graves' shirt, ripping the dirty material away from his body. He cut through Graves' belt and slit the pants, leaving the negro naked except for his boots. A wrinkled old woman scuttled close, reaching out to clutch Graves' genitals. She howled with laughter as the Comanchero screamed and urinated.

Then the braves kicked Graves' feet from under him and lashed him down where John Bear's body had been.

Eleanor Dalton was brought forward to stand between the negro's spread legs. Two women held her while a third pulled the doeskin dress over her head. She tried to cover her nudity, but the squaws pushed her hands away, forcing her to display her body to the watching Indians and the spreadeagled negro. Graves moaned and became erect. It was purely instinctive, an involuntary reaction born of fear, near madness and the sight of the woman's lithe, full-breasted figure.

Iron Knife laughed and shouted to the squaws. They shrieked, broad, sadistic grins appearing on their faces.

Roughly, they dragged Eleanor Dalton between Graves' legs, forcing her to straddle him. Then they began to push her down. She groaned, shaking her head as she realised what they planned, but the women shoved their feet against her knees, bending her legs so that she squatted over the negro's manhood. A third squaw came forward and reached between the prisoners, grasping the Comanchero's erection as the others leant heavily on the white woman's shoulders.

Eleanor Dalton screamed as Graves entered her. His upward motion was pure reflex, an atavistic compulsion that had little to do with desire. It was the same animal reaction that drove his hips up, back, and up again, ramming into the woman crouched over him.

At first she moaned and tried to pull back, gritting her teeth as the squaws held her in position. But then, slowly, a kind of madness came over her as, against her will, she became aroused. Her lips parted and her head lolled back. Slowly, she began to move her hips, grinding down against the negro's thrusts. Her movements grew faster, urgent, and a thread of spittle dribbled from her open mouth. Her eyes closed and she began to whimper, matching Graves stroke for stroke.

The squaws fell back, watching with sly smiles as the two prisoners approached a climax.

Eleanor Dalton screamed, her pale hair tumbling in the firelight as her head shook and she took Graves into her. The negro grunted, humping upwards as he spent himself, and fell back.

Around them, the Comanches howled their approval.

Abruptly, the woman threw herself to one side, disgust replacing desire. She began to weep.

Iron Knife grinned and tossed a small skinning knife to her.

'Now kill him.'

From where he watched, Gunn could sense that the woman's mood had changed. Lust had ruled her body, prompting actions that now filled her with self-hate. It was clear in her wild, glaring eyes as she stared at the knife, and for a moment he wondered if she would kill herself. Then the emotion became directed outwards at the man who had aroused her, and she turned to Graves with a feral light in her eyes.

Graves saw it and shuddered. Then screamed as the knife traced a bloody line down his stomach. He gagged as she seized his genitals, staring at them over the knife.

'Jesus Christ!' He was almost too scared to get the words out. 'Listen to me, lady. I got a gun hidden in my boot. Cut my hands free an' I'll finish it fast fer both of us.'

He said it low and fast, hoping the words would penetrate the woman's madness. They seemed to, for she slowed the downward swoop of the blade, stroking it over his stomach as she glanced up.

'You *had* me.' Outrage sounded in her voice, abruptly replaced by a coy wonderment. 'I never had a black man before.'

Graves realised that she was mad, and tried to penetrate her derangement.

'The gun, lady! I got a derringer in my boot. Cut my hands free an' I can get us both out o' this.'

Eleanor Dalton giggled and twisted around, throwing herself full-length over Graves' body. She writhed against him, pressing her lips down on his mouth as she reached up towards his wrist.

'Yes,' she muttered, 'yes. Kill me.'

And she cut the ropes.

It happened almost too fast for Gunn to follow. He saw the woman reach up, the knife slash to right and left, then she was rolling aside and the negro was coming up to a sitting position. He stretched, fumbling at his right leg. And Gunn saw the derringer.

The woman lifted to a kneeling posture, but the negro shoved her aside, shouting something as he levelled the little gun at the Comanche chief.

A thrown hatchet caught his shoulder as he fired, spoiling his aim so that the bullet flew wide into the watching Comanches. An Indian screamed and went down, forgotten in the rush towards the prisoner. The derringer barked once more, and Gunn powered forwards.

He didn't see the second bullet hit Little Buffalo, and he couldn't see the negro anymore through the milling warriors. But he had the diversion he needed.

Shoving through the crowd of screaming Comanches, he kicked a fire, scattering flames over a nearby tepee. The dry hide caught instantly, adding to the confusion, and Gunn reached the white woman. He grabbed her arm, yanking her upright and hauled her back through the crowd. A woman yelled something at him and he clubbed her down. A brave appeared in his path and he shoved the Winchester into the man's stomach and squeezed the trigger, blowing the warrior backwards.

The camp was in uproar, the fire spreading fast from lodge to lodge. Gunn ran through the flames, dragging Eleanor Dalton with him. The Comanches were too intent for the moment on killing Graves and dousing the fires to notice the escape, and the few who did, died as they tried to stop Gunn.

He made for the pony herd and lifted the woman bodily onto a pinto mustang. He swung up behind her and kicked the animal to a gallop.

Two warriors blocked his path as he thundered through the close-packed tepees and he rode them down, driving the pony headlong into them before either could fire the rifles they carried. Then he was out of the camp and riding hard for the bluff where Abrams waited.

Samuel Graves never knew how he helped save Eleanor Dalton. His actions were prompted by hatred and raw anger at losing money on his deal with Iron Knife. When he drew the hidden derringer his only thought had been to kill the Comanche war chief and then himself. When he saw the first shot go wild he fired again without thinking. After that his world exploded in a haze of red as the enraged Indians descended upon him.

When they finally pulled back, all that was left recognisable were Graves' boots.

Iron Knife stood over the ravaged corpse, his own hatchet bloody, and looked around for the woman. When he realised that she was gone he sent warriors through the camp, searching. They found no trace of the woman, but they reported three men dead, and a squaw. One man was shot, the others trampled, and Iron Knife bellowed his anger as he realised that his prisoner had been taken from him.

Within minutes those warriors not fighting the fire that

raged through the camp were mounted, heading out in search of the woman.

Matthew Gunn made straight for the hide-out. The night was dark enough to make tracking difficult, and he wanted to put as much distance as possible between himself and the Comanches. The fire he had started would keep some of the braves busy, but he was reasonably sure that a fair proportion would be out looking for him before very long.

The rescued woman wasn't making things easy. The hysteria that had gripped her after the forced seduction was still with her, and she struggled, trying to break free. Gunn wasted no time arguing with her; instead, he simply punched her and held her, unconscious, across the mustang's shoulders.

They reached the bluff and he halted the pony, handing the supine woman down to Abrams. The Ranger captain took her without speaking, carrying her into the shelter of the cleft. Gunn tethered the mustang, tying a folded blanket over its back in lieu of a saddle, and followed Abrams into cover. The Ranger was already pulling a shirt over the woman's nudity, working fast as she began to come round. He got a pair of spare pants on her before she woke and slapped a hand over her mouth when she opened it to scream.

Her eyes were wide, staring at Gunn, and she began to tremble violently.

'It's alright, ma'am,' murmured Abrams, 'you're safe now. He's white. We're gonna take you home.'

Gradually, her trembling eased and she clutched at the Ranger, hiding her face against his chest. He turned towards Gunn.

'What happened back there?'

'I'll tell you on the way,' grunted the halfbreed, pulling on his shirt. 'But for a while things looked kind of black.'

CHAPTER TWELVE

They rode due north through a night filled with menace, each rock, every cactus assuming the shape of a Comanche warrior. The pale moon threw only a fitful light over the Staked Plains, but to the three fugitives it seemed bright as the noon sun. Gunn lead the way, taking them up onto the rimrock where the ground was harder and their trail wouldn't show so clearly. He meandered deliberately, seeking to confuse any pursuit, taking them off the bluff into the desert with reluctance.

On his own, he could have lost the Comanches. Burdened with the woman, he gave them a fifty-fifty chance that would reduce to zero if they were spotted.

Eleanor Dalton was still halfway hysterical, her strained mind fighting to adjust to her ordeal, to the shock of self-knowledge that had possessed her after her wanton episode with Graves. Gunn put her on his own horse, using his lariat to tie her in the saddle, where she rode like an automaton. Abrams stationed himself behind her, ready to goad her on if she faltered, but she kept pace, mumbling softly to herself.

Around dawn there was a light rain. It didn't last long, but Gunn took the opportunity to wash the dye from his hair and body. It seemed to reassure the woman, for she became quieter, less nervous of the hard-faced man guiding them through the badlands.

They halted beneath a blazing sun that shone from directly above them, baking the sand and bathing them in their own sweat. Gunn rationed the water, giving most of it to the horses. Then he fed them their first meal in twelve hours: he had deliberately starved the animals for fear of leaving droppings to mark their trail. After that they pushed on.

Back at the bluff a party of Comanches found the cooled-off remnants of the fire and the marks of three horses. Four of the Indians scouted ahead, while the fifth set off to find Iron Knife.

The war chief reached the bluff with twenty men, and took off at a gallop along the cold trail.

He was angry, consumed with a cold fury that demanded blood and suffering to slake his thirst for vengeance. His defeat at the Flying D had eroded his authority over the gathered bands of Nemmenna, and he had sought to use the captured woman to strengthen the loyalty of his followers. Her disappearance, and the fire in the village, had shaken his position badly, and even now groups of warriors were drifting away. Iron Knife was determined to get the woman back – and kill whoever had taken her.

Nolan and Christie reached the Flying D on played-out horses. They found Dalton's surviving hands rebuilding the ranch. The stone and adobe that constituted the bulk of the place had withstood the fire with only black burn marks to show what had happened. The timber of the main door, the central room, and the interior veranda had suffered worse damage, but already the house was regaining a semblance of order.

They rode in with a story prepared to account for Dalton's absence.

Josh Whitney, the foreman, wanted to hear it as soon as they dismounted. He called a hand to take their horses, and hurried them inside the building.

'What happened? Where's Nat?'

'Dead,' said Nolan flatly. At least that much was true. 'Got killed on the way to the Comanch' village.'

'How?' Whitney had been with Dalton from the beginning; he was a friend as much as a foreman, and there was something about these two he didn't like.

'Well,' Nolan said slowly, sensing Whitney's animosity, 'we headed fer the village with the 'breed showin' us the way. Then the injuns jumped us. Abrams an' the 'breed cut off on their own, figgerin' to bring the woman out, an' the rest of us headed south fer Abilene.

'We had to fort up because the Comanch' was thicker'n fleas on a dog, an' Dalton reckoned the three of us would stand a better chance than a big party.'

'You said Abrams an' Gunn was ridin' fer the village,' interrupted Whitney.

'Yeah, sure.' Nolan nodded agreement. 'But you know how Dalton felt about his wife.'

He shrugged eloquently, and Whitney grunted.

'So,' continued Nolan, 'he asked Jude an' me to cut loose an' ride back. We left the Rangers to handle themselves an' moved out in the night. We was makin' fer where we thought the village to be located when the injuns hit us.'

He paused dramatically, fixing a sympathetic expression on his face.

'It was a runnin' fight. The three o' us against about fifteen injuns. Dalton got hit. We did our best to keep him in the saddle, but he was too bad hurt. After a while he died on us, an' we had to run fer it.'

'Poor ole Dalton,' added Christie. 'Them Comanch' just rode him down. Was that saved us, I reckon. They was so busy stompin' him down that we got clear away.'

Christie's fingers were getting itchy from the thought of the gold eagles hidden by the fountain. He was, at the best of times, an unsubtle man, more used to using a Colt than his brains. But there were too many cowhands around the spread to risk a gunfight. It looked as though a fair number of the Flying D riders had been on the open range when the Comanches attacked, and come in after the fight, swelling the force already in the ranch house.

Anyway, there were too many to handle, so Christie decided to leave things to Nolan.

The dark man was doing enough thinking for both of them. His story sounded plausible enough, and there was no way Whitney could disprove it, even though the foreman looked doubtful. The random factors were something else. Gunn and the Ranger captain might come back with the woman; or the survivors of the Ranger Company – if there were any – might appear; getting the money was a big enough problem in itself; getting out of the territory was another. Nolan decided to bide his time, at least until dark.

Iron Knife was too impatient to wait. He lost the trail on a section of bedrock twenty miles north of the big camp and called his scouts in. There was no way of telling exactly where the fugitives were headed, but given that the woman had come from the ranch, it seemed safe to assume they would go back there.

The Comanche war chief turned his pony and rode for the Flying D.

Matthew Gunn faced a difficult choice: the Dalton spread was the nearest white enclave, but it couldn't take the Comanches long to guess that for themselves. That meant the horse warriors could get between him and the ranch; Amarillo, Pecos and Abilene – the closest towns – were days distant across hostile country. Nolan and Christie had been riding for Abilene, but Gunn had given his word that he would rescue the woman. Bringing her safe to home could mean that Abrams would use his influence to drop the murder charge outstanding in Texas, leaving Gunn free to come and go as he pleased. Renege on his promise, and he would still be wanted; fulfil it, and the men he hunted might get free.

Not for the first time the halfbreed found his conscience divided. He chose to put the matter in the hands of whichever gods ruled the Staked Plains, and asked Abrams.

'Hell,' grunted the Ranger, 'I was kinda figgerin' on you settin' the path. Nat could be back on the D by now. Amarillo's two days off, the ranch ain't more'n one; let's try fer there.'

Gunn shrugged and turned west.

They were twenty miles out when the Comanches showed again.

Gunn saw them first, a line of men walking their ponies along the crest of the ridge to his right. He looked to his left, and saw a second line. Glancing behind, he watched the Indians close ranks, so that he was riding at the centre of a fan of horsemen.

Then they closed ahead. Gunn reined in: there was no point in trying anything else.

Behind him, Eleanor Dalton muffled a scream and Abrams cursed. Gunn twisted on the blanket saddle, motioning for silence.

'They want the woman first.' His voice was harsh with urgency. 'Let me talk to them. Maybe I can work something out.'

It was a pretty slender thread on which to hang their lives, but at that moment it was all they had – and hope was better than nothing. He remembered something his father had once told him: *A gun is a tool, Matt, nothing more. Times are, your life will depend on using it right. But more often than not, you can use your tongue better. Get a man talking and you might be able to out-fox him; if that doesn't work, then use the gun.*

He was thinking hard along just those lines as three Comanches broke from the ranks and came towards him.

The lead rider was tall for an Indian, a big, well-muscled man on a paint pony. He carried a new model Winchester and the black-tipped eagle feathers of his war bonnet numbered better than thirty coups. Gunn knew this must be the paramount chief of the gathered Nemmenna.

The Comanche halted his mustang and sat for long seconds in silence. Then he spoke, moving his hands in the sign-talk of the South-western deserts.

'I am Iron Knife, leader of all Nemmenna. You have taken the woman from me and I shall kill you for that, but you are a brave man for doing it and I shall place your hair high on my trophy pole.'

Gunn answered fast, anxious to catch the Comanche's interest before he was cut down.

'I am called Matthew Gunn by the white people, but my mother's folk called me Azul. My mother was Apache a daughter of the Chiricahua.'

Iron Knife grunted, and a whisper of surprise rose from the watching Indians. Gunn fought to retain the psychological initiative.

'Your people and mine are old enemies, but we share one thing: the white men have taken our land.'

'That is true,' said Iron Knife, curious.

'My people have fought to the west and to the south,' continued Gunn, 'and fight still. My father's blood was white, but he lived amongst the Chiricahua and raised me in the country of the lonely hills, as an Apache warrior.'

'Hya!' Iron Knife's cry was half grudging approval. 'It is good! No white man could have come among us to take the woman. When I kill you, I shall honour your body.'

'*If* you kill me!' Gunn shouted, gambling three lives on the war chief's conceit. 'For I challenge you to single combat.'

An Apache would have laughed at the challenge and shot him out of his saddle, spitting on the corpse for its foolishness. But the Comanches were not so practical, their society was based upon a tight system of honour and valour. And Iron Knife's dream of uniting the scattered bands to drive the whites from the plains depended heavily on his personal authority. The challenge was an invitation he could not afford to refuse.

'So,' he shouted, pitching his own voice so that his warriors would hear clearly, 'you challenge me. What if you win?'

'We ride free,' said Gunn, 'and your people will let us pass.'

'It is fair,' replied Iron Knife, 'but it will never be. I shall fight you now and I shall kill you, and then I shall kill your white friend and take the woman back.'

'If you can,' grunted the halfbreed.

Iron Knife turned, shouting to his warriors, and they closed around the trio, studying Gunn with curious eyes and more than a little respect. Few men had challenged the war chief, and fewer still had lived.

Abrams watched the Indians closing in, keeping his hands ostentatiously away from his guns. He reached across to seize Eleanor Dalton's bridle in case the woman should panic, then called out to Gunn.

'What's goin' on?'

'I invited their chief to a fight,' explained the halfbreed. 'If I win, we go free.'

'Do I need to ask what happens if you lose?' Abrams murmured.

Gunn shook his head.

The two men flanking Iron Knife herded the Ranger and the woman off to one side as the other Comanches backed their ponies to form a long avenue of around four hundred yards depth, and one hundred in width. Iron Knife called out in his own language and a brave handed Gunn a war lance. The halfbreed took the ten-foot pole, weighing it in his hand. It was not a weapon with which he was familiar, for the Apache preferred to fight with bow, or rifle, using hatchet and knife for close work; but there was no choice to the matter. Iron Knife was already backing his pony off, lining it for the charge.

Gunn walked his animal back to the farther end of the avenue, hefting the unnaccustomed weight of the lance in his right hand.

Iron Knife held his pole two thirds of the way down the shaft, nestling it tight between elbow and ribs so that the metal-headed tip angled slightly downwards. Gunn copied him. The Comanche shouted something, dancing his pony in a tight circle, and the halfbreed guessed that he was boasting to his followers. Gunn removed his stetson and tossed it over to Abrams, then waited.

Iron Knife screamed a war cry and heeled his pony forwards, Gunn rammed his boots against the mustang's ribs and went to meet the charging rider.

They thundered at one another, the war ponies hitting full gallop in yards. Iron Knife's lance dropped level with Gunn's knees, lifting as they closed. It was the classic Comanche gut-thrust, the lance aimed at the enemy's groin, where it would do the most damage, lifting him off his horse dead or crippled, but leaving the victor clear to haul the pole free from torn entrails.

Had it connected as Iron Knife planned, Gunn would have been a dead man.

But he saw the thrust coming and tilted to the side. He slid across and over the pony, using his right arm and leg to hold himself in position along the animal's left flank.

Iron Knife's lance drew blood from the mustang, but left Gunn unhurt.

The halfbreed swung back onto the saddle and turned the beast in its own length. For all his speed, Iron Knife was faster. The Comanche was coming back even as Gunn turned, the lance angling for a second thrust.

Gunn feinted to the left, counting on Iron Knife anticipating the motion, and swung upright as the lance moved to counter his manoeuvre. It tore his shirt, but his chest crossed the stroke so that the weight of his body hit the pole even as his own weapon drove for the Comanche's belly.

Iron Knife sucked in his stomach, hurling himself sideways as he raised his lance to deflect Gunn's blow. Both men felt their arms forced upwards, and Gunn felt a heavy blow along the side of his head as his lance dragged back over the Comanche's body.

Sharp metal cut his temple and warm blood spilled down his face, but he was clear and moving towards the end of the tilting ground.

He hauled the mustang round for the third run and saw Iron Knife already charging down on him. They met and Gunn saw too late that the Indian's tactics were changed. The lance dropped and he shifted aside, but this time it stayed down. He heeled the pony over, yanking hard on the guide rein, but the animal was moving too fast to change its direction quickly enough, and the lance hit.

It slammed hard into the mustang's chest, driving deep through lungs and heart, and the pony screamed, blowing spumes of blood over the sand. Its knees buckled and its head went down. Gunn felt the withers rise and pitched himself forwards over the fallen head.

Iron Knife's lance snapped as the pony fell against the shaft, but he reached out and snatched Gunn's pole as he went past.

A great shout rose from the watching Comanches as their chief swung his mount around and the halfbreed tumbled onto the sand.

Eleanor Dalton screamed as she watched Gunn hit the ground and Iron Knife adjust the captured lance for another charge. Abrams let his right hand drift slowly towards his Colt, swearing softly as he calculated how many Indians he could down before they killed him. After using one shot on the woman he reckoned he could take at least three Comanches with him.

Gunn landed on his left shoulder and rolled with the fall. Propelled by the momentum of the dying pony, he tumbled end over end, tasting sand in his mouth as he twisted and came up onto his knees and hands. He looked up and saw Iron Knife coming in fast with the lance pointed at his belly. He came to his feet, powering sideways as the Comanche went past. The pony's shoulder hit him in the chest, slamming him down again. But the lance had missed.

Iron Knife turned, and whooped, and came on at full gallop.

Gunn stood with his legs spread, knees braced to take the impact of the lance. He crouched slightly, holding both hands before him as though to fend off the sharp metal tip.

His pale blue eyes were fixed on the glinting spear and his ears were deaf to Iron Knife's victorious yell.

The Comanche closed the distance between them with ferocious speed. His lance was aimed at the centre of Gunn's stomach and his eyes were alight with savage joy, anticipating his opponent's death.

Gunn poised on the balls of his feet, bringing his left leg slightly to the front. His battle-honed senses took in the direction of the Comanche's charge, the angle of the lance, the speed of the mustang. As the metal tip shafted at his belly, he pivoted on both feet, leaning back so that the pole brushed past his midriff.

And he reached out to take it in both hands.

He swung his body, throwing his whole weight against the lance, dragging it round to yank back Iron Knife's hand, slam the butt hard across the Comanche's spine.

The move took the war chief by surprise. Suddenly the easy target was gone, taking the lance. He felt a blow against his lower back and shifted sideways, trying hard to retain his grip on the weapon. It was a bad mistake, for it lost him his balance on the pony, and when he tried to regain the saddle the lance flailed into him and he crashed to the ground.

Gunn moved fast, ramming the butt of the lance into Iron Knife's ribs before the Comanche could roll clear. The war chief grunted as air gusted from his lungs, and tried to push to his feet. Gunn used the lance like a staff, whacking it down across his enemy's shoulders. Iron Knife's arms gave under the blow and he collapsed face down on the sand.

Gunn shifted his grip, taking the lance in both hands halfway down the shaft. He planted his feet on either side of the Comanche's body and raised his arms high above his head. Then, putting all the power of his muscular shoulders into the blow, he brought the lance down.

The edged metal head clove through the skin between Iron Knife's shoulderblades, and the coppery flesh was suddenly dark with blood. It sliced through a lung, grated on a rib, and imbedded deep in the sand.

Iron Knife screamed, his body arching backwards against the pain. His legs flailed as though he was trying to push himself clear of the lance, and his wildly scrabbling hands gouged great chunks of sand from the ground. He writhed and struggled like some great insect pinned down on a collector's board, and he lifted his contorted face to the sky, opening his mouth to scream again. But only blood came out, and he shuddered and died.

From around the battle ground, lifting from more than twenty Comanche throats, there came a wild, wailing cry. It ululated over the empty land, a keening that was both a death song for the fallen chief and a lament for a lost dream. Iron Knife's vision died with him, and his followers knew it. There was no other Comanche strong enough to hold the bands together, no other warrior gifted with the medicine dream; the braves mourned a dead comrade and a lost hope.

Matthew Gunn stood in silence, his face impassive waiting for the warriors to finish their lament.

They fell silent and a man rode forward. He took the rein of Iron Knife's mustang and held it out to Gunn. Then, using sign language, he began to speak.

'You have beaten Iron Knife, who was a great warrior. You have proved yourself mightier in battle, and all that was Iron Knife's is now yours. You are free to go, as our chief promised.

If you wish it, I will take you to our camp where you will see what is now yours.'

Gunn stared gravely at the man. 'I will take the pony, but that is all. The horses of your chief, his weapons, his lodge and his wives, I trust to you to share amongst the Nemmenna. Tell your people that it is my wish that it be so.'

He glanced down at the bloodied body of the war chief. Flies were already clustering around the shaft protruding from its back.

'Take the body of Iron Knife with you. He was a brave warrior and a mighty chief and it is my wish that you should bury him with honour, as befits a war chief of the Nemmenna.'

'It is good,' nodded the Comanche, and called out to the others.

Gunn watched as four horsemen dismounted, walking over to the corpse. They pulled the lance free of the body, disturbing the flies so that they buzzed irritably, trying to get back to their feast. Then, solemnly, the warriors lifted Iron Knife and carried him to their waiting ponies. Two braves gave up their lances and a travois was rigged. They set the body upon the thing and mounted. The Indian who had first spoken turned back to Gunn.

'Go now, in peace. You and your companions. We shall not harm you.' He paused, his face stoney. 'But know this Azul, who is called Matthew Gunn: when next we meet, I shall kill you.'

He turned his mustang, falling into step beside the animal dragging the travois, and called out to the waiting men. Silently, they rode away, leaving the halfbreed and his two companions alone in the badlands.

Gunn waited until they were gone from sight lost in the shimmering haze lifting up from the sand. Then he swung astride Iron Knife's pony, grinning at Abrams.

'We're safe to go now. They won't try to stop us.'

Abrams let a whistle shrill from between clenched teeth.

'That,' he said softly, 'was about as close as I like to part my hair. Thank God you beat him.'

'It was the talk that did it,' replied Gunn, poker-faced. 'After that it was just a question of making sure he got the point.'

CHAPTER THIRTEEN

Josh Whitney had a sneaky feeling the two hardcases were planning something. What it might be, he couldn't guess, but they gave him an itchy feeling he didn't like. Their story of the Comanche attack and Nat Dalton's death sounded plausible enough – but Josh didn't believe it. There was no real reason why he shouldn't, except the feeling seated deep in his guts that they were lying. And that made him edgy.

Josh had drifted around Texas and New Mexico since he ran away from home when he was thirteen. He had done a little Indian trading, worked the ranches as a hired hand, and then enlisted with the Confederacy when the War Between The States broke out. At Vicksburg, he had met Nat Dalton, a young lieutenant like himself, and they had hit it off from the start. Nat's dream of a cattle kingdom in west Texas had caught his imagination, and he had joined his friend in the ride west as soon as his discharge papers came through. Together they had built the Flying D into the finest spread in two hundred miles of rough country. Nat's marriage had come as no great surprise to Josh, though he had never really taken to the uppity Eastern girl in her high-falutin' ways, and sly betrayals. Josh had known all about her affair with Billy-Joe McAllister, but had resisted the impulse to tell his friend about it: Nat would have been hurt too bad. Instead, Josh had settled the matter in his own way. The young cowboy had laughed off his warnings, confident of his standing with Eleanor, and gone on romancing Nat's wife. So Josh had let the herd run that stormy night, and when the right moment showed itself his boot had hooked Billy-Joe from his saddle and left him smeared over a quarter mile of prairie.

It was the same kind of loyalty to Nat – or his memory – that got Josh out of bed at dawn and sent him prowling round to the room where Nolan and Christie were sleeping.

Except they weren't.

When Josh rounded the pile of timbers that was all that was left of the veranda, he saw the Southerner hauling slabs clear of the fountain. Christie was giggling as he lifted bags of wash-leather into sight, tugging the draw-strings to let bright, gold coins spill over his dirty boots.

Josh watched them fall, hauling a .40 calibre Remington out of the worn holster slung cross-ways on his left hip.

He lifted the old gun and thumbed the hammer back. It hadn't be used on a man since the Civil War, and he smiled to himself as he lined the muzzle on Christie's back.

A cock crowed, drowning out the *click* of the hammer. The bird's raucous cry also served to cover the footsteps behind him.

The steps were made by Nolan's boots as he catfooted from the shadows, and the first Josh knew about them was when the business end of a Colt dug a furrow in his back. He kept his own gun pointed at Christie as he twisted his neck round far enough to see the man standing behind him.

'Looks like a Mexican stand-off, mister.' He put more conviction into his voice than he felt. 'You gun me, an' yore friend gets one where it hurts.'

'Go ahead.' Nolan's voice was flat, cold as a high plains winter. 'You're dead together.'

Christie let a bag fall, ignoring the coins tinkling over the courtyard as he stared around at Whitney. His mouth fell open and his hand moved part-way to his Colt. Then it stopped as he saw the black hole of the Remington's barrel pointing at his chest.

He looked over Whitney's shoulder into Nolan's eyes, and saw nothing there.

'Oh, Jesus!' His voice was harsh with urgency. 'Do something, Nolan.'

'Sure, Jude,' said the dark man, 'I'll kill him. 'Course that means you get one, too. You want that, Jude?'

'No!' Christie shook his head vigorously. 'No. Don't.'

Nolan smiled. There was no humour in the movement of his face, only a cold, death-like calculation that sent shivers of sudden fear along Christie's spine. Whitney stood with the Remington still aimed at the Southerner, his grizzled face set in an expression of fatalistic determination.

He had made up his mind to kill them both when he saw the blond man hauling the eagles from the hiding place. Now he knew he could only get one, but that was better than none; so he reckoned on gunning Christie before Nolan killed him. His only regret was that Nat Dalton had never seen fit to tell him about the hidden hoard of gold.

He died with the thought fixed forever in his mind.

From over his shoulder, Nolan stared at Christie, moving his head slightly to indicate that the blond man should move to the side. Christie caught the movement and grinned.

Josh saw the look and began to turn his head. His aim wavered slightly, shifting off to one side, and Christie grabbed the opportunity to get himself out from under the gun. He ducked, hurling himself bodily across the courtyard, hoping Nolan was still as fast as ever.

The foreman saw the blond man move, and cursed his own indecision, even as he triggered the Remington. The bullet blasted chips of stone from the ornamental surround of the fountain, flaking shards of granite over Christie's tumbling body.

Whitney saw the bullet miss. And felt Nolan's hit. For an instant of protracted time he felt the agony wash through his body as the .45 calibre slug blasted his rib cage. It exploded a kidney, opened the lining of his stomach, and exited in a spray of crimson froth that left blood over the coins, spilled around the fountain. Josh Whitney saw the gold turn to red as he fell face-down onto the eagles. He stared close-range at the embossed figures decorating the coins, and thought – irrelevently – that he had never been so close to so much money in his life. A blind-eyed bird stared back at him and he opened his mouth to chuckle at the blank expression on its face.

It seemed amusing that a small circle of metal could be worth so much. Then he saw the coin wash red, and realised that the colour was coming from his mouth. He watched the indentations of the metal catch the blood and fill, spilling over the raised engravure work, and drip off onto the dew-wet stone of the courtyard.

Then his eyes glazed and the sight went away, and there was only red. Followed by the blackness.

Nolan swung his gun around to cover the cowhands spilling out of the surrounding rooms. Christie climbed to his feet with a Colt in his hand, stooped over Whitney's corpse, and came up with the Remington. Between them, they held the Flying D hands at bay.

'Stay still!' Nolan's voice cut like a whiplash through the dawn air. 'Ain't no reason fer anyone else to get killed.'

His air of command – and the levelled guns – stopped the cowboys in their tracks. They stood in varying attitudes of surprise, most part-dressed against the possibility of a further Indian attack, but none ready to risk going up against the two men holding the cocked guns.

Outside the ranch house the cockerel brayed his call for the second time.

'Get the money, Jude.' Nolan's voice was cold and confident. 'Ain't no use to stayin' around anymore.'

'Right.'

Christie holstered his own gun and held the Remington ready to use as he scooped coins back into the sacks.

No-one tried to stop them: cowboys were hired to tend cattle, not chance their lives against hardnose gunhands. And with both the boss and the foreman dead, there didn't seem too much point in defending the Flying D anymore. So the hired men just stood immobile, watching Christie scoop more money than most of them would see in their entire lives into the soft leather bags.

By the time the Southerner was finished, he had six sacks spread around his feet and Whitney's blood all over his hands. He giggled, wiping the viscous mess on the foreman's shirt, and looked up at Nolan.

'Got it. What now?'

'What you think?' Nolan said it without shifting his gaze from the watching cowhands. 'We get the hell outta here.'

Christie grinned and lifted three of the bags. He passed them to Nolan who draped them over one shoulder. The Southerner picked up the others, and together the two killers backed out of the courtyard.

Nolan let Christie go through into the main building first, then called over his shoulder.

'Jude, there's a scattergun in there someplace. Check it's loaded and pass it to me.'

Christie did as he was told, holding the shotgun ready to use while he waited for Nolan to holster the Colt and take the heavier weapon. Nolan levelled the twin barrels of the gun on the watching hands, and smiled.

'Anyone tries to stop us gets dead fast.'

'Fast as you?'

The voice was flat, cold and full of hate. It belonged to Matthew Gunn.

CHAPTER FOURTEEN

He came out of the shadows, a tall man with hate in his eyes and death riding the Colt in his hand. Dried blood caked one side of his face, and his long, pale hair was a sticky mixture of blood and dust. Abrams stood behind and to one side of him, a cocked Colt pointed at Christie's belly.

Nolan didn't turn.

'I got two barrels pointed at these men.' His voice was almost casual. 'Both o' them got a full load o' ten-gauge shot. You try anythin', an' most o' them are gonna be suddenly dead.'

'So?' Gunn's voice was as dismissive as Nolan's. 'I don't know them. You're the one I want. You and Christie. And you're dead whatever.'

'No!' Abrams' voice was harsh in the silent room. 'You can't Gunn.'

'Why the hell not?'

'Jesus Christ! What are you? You'd trade all o' those men fer them two?'

'Sure.' Gunn's voice was cold, certain. 'I came a long way to find them. Now I got them, I'm going to kill them.'

'Not while I'm here.' Abrams sounded torn, but his gun still swung to cover the halfbreed. 'You fire an' I'll kill you.'

'Well now, ain't that nice.' Nolan's voice was mocking. 'What you gonna do boy? Drop me an' die yoreself? Or you gonna let me walk outta here an' chance findin' me later?'

Gunn's finger took up trigger slack. His Colt held rock-steady on the base of Nolan's spine, where the column of bone tags on to the pelvic girdle.

'You're a dead man, Nolan.' He ignored the gun he could feel at his own back. 'I can get you and Christie before anyone stops me. That's the difference: I'm ready to take the gamble.'

'Don't make me do it!' Abrams' voice was a harsh plea. 'Fer God's sake, Gunn, don't force me to kill you.'

'Sorry Abrams.' The man called Gunn sounded calm as a preacher at a Sunday picnic. 'But I made a promise a long time ago. I'm not about to forget it.'

'Oh, fuck.' Abrams' tone was abruptly despairing, divided between friendship and duty. 'You loose off an' I'm bounden to kill you.'

'Go ahead,' said Gunn. 'You can't do it fast enough to stop me.'

He tensed, readying himself for the bullet in the back, calculating that he could down Nolan and spin to take Christie before Abrams' shot killed him. He had no doubt but that the Ranger would carry out his unwilling promise anymore than he had doubts about his own determination to kill the scalp-hunters. It wasn't the way he wanted it: he had hoped to take them singly, slowly, the way he had killed the others. He wanted them to know why they were dying, to think about it as they suffered. But now, with both in killing range, he could no more let them go than he could stop hunting them.

He took a deep breath and prepared to die.

Eleanor Dalton ended the stand-off with a wild shriek and a sudden movement.

Since getting back to the ranch, she had stood quiet, gazing vacantly around her as though seeking some familiar land-mark that was no longer there. Now – madly – she recognised Nolan and went to him.

She shoved Abrams aside with the strength of the demented, pushed Gunn off balance, and threw herself on Nolan. Her arms swung round to hold him as she buried her face against his back, weeping and mumbling as she clutched at him. Her arms encircled him, pushing the shotgun down, and Nolan cursed, spinning to drag her loose. The crazy woman clung like a limpet, interposing her body between Gunn and her lover.

'Nolan, Nolan!' her voice was a frantic wail. 'I've come back. Darling, we can go away. We'll leave here. Together. You and me. No-one else.'

Christie made to move, but Abrams' gun swung to cover him, and the Texas Ranger's eyes said *no* as clearly as words.

Around the courtyard, the cowhands found cover faster than jackrabbits with a hawk in the air. They disappeared into the rooms like gophers hitting their burrows, glad to be clear of the scattergun and its menacing promise.

Matthew Gunn stood, angry and frustrated, watching his quarry try to shake the woman loose.

Nolan kept hold of the shotgun and backed hard against a wall. Eleanor Dalton took the force of the blow and gasped, her arms falling away from the dark man's shoulders. Nolan dropped to a crouch, levelling the shotgun at the blond-haired halfbreed, and reached back to grab the woman.

He dragged her across his chest and tilted the shotgun so that it pointed at her skull.

'Alright, Breed. You want me, you come an' get me.'

Gunn's Colt lifted. His arm extended out in a straight, rock-steady line, from his chest. The hammer was back on full cock and his eyes were pale and blue and cold as they sighted down the barrel. Most of Nolan's body was covered by the woman, and Gunn's aim held the Colt on her chest. At that range the .45 calibre bullet would penetrate her body and still kill Nolan.

'Well?' The dark man grinned, confident of his advantage. 'You gonna kill the woman to get me?'

'Yes,' said Matthew Gunn. And squeezed the trigger.

CHAPTER FIFTEEN

Something hard and heavy and solid slammed against the back of his skull, and he heard the gun go off knowing the shot was flying wild. The floor lifted up to meet his face and he heard Nolan laugh.

His teeth mashed over his tongue and he spat blood, fighting to hold onto consciousness as pain filled the inside of his head and nausea roiled through his guts.

He tasted blood from his bitten tongue and dust from the floor. Slowly, each movement a long, painful action that demanded more power than his body seemed to hold, he thumbed back the hammer of the Colt and twisted around, pushing up off the dirty floor.

Waves of redness danced across his eyes and he blinked, trying to focus on the figures moving around him. He spotted a black-clad shape and guessed it was Nolan. He lifted the Colt with both hands, but something hit him again and he went away into a darkness blacker than the hard, cold anger that filled his being along with the pain.

The floor came up to hit him again and he grunted and fell back.

Abrams shifted the Colt to cover the two men heading for the door. Nolan still held the shotgun against Eleanor Dalton's head, and Christie had a gun pointed at the Ranger.

'You won't get far.' Abrams knew it would make no difference speaking to them, but it might – just – stop the two guns from going off. 'Whole territory's crawlin' with Comanche. If they don't get you, the Rangers will.'

'Mister.' Nolan's voice bit like a knife through the warm butter of the morning's air. 'If you weren't a Ranger I'd kill you here an' now. Things bein' equal, I'll take the woman. Try comin' after us, an' she's dead.'

He grinned like a wolverine on a fresh-dug grave.

'Thanks fer stoppin' the 'breed. He'd have shot me if you hadn't clubbed him.'

'Yeah,' grunted Abrams, wondering if he should have left Gunn to open fire.

He let his Colt drop to the floor and watched the two men exit. Nolan still holding the woman like a shield across his body.

He heard them climb onto their horses, then listened to them driving off the remaining mounts. A shot blew splinters from the door-frame as they galloped away, persuading him to stay under cover until the sound of the hoof-beats was gone into the emptiness of the Staked Plains.

Then he turned to Matthew Gunn.

The halfbreed had no right to be on his feet so soon: Abrams' blow had been a heavy one, prompted by desperation and the sure knowledge that Gunn would risk his own life and anyone else's to get Nolan and Christie. But the man was up and moving, fumbling dazedly for his Colt, checking the load as he moved to the door.

'They're gone.' Abrams' voice sounded suddenly tired, sad. 'They ran off the horses. You won't catch them.'

The eyes that looked back at him closed his mouth tighter than a solid gulp of bad firewater. He wondered why people thought of black as the colour of death: looking at Matthew Gunn's blue eyes, he knew that was how death looked when it stared into your face. Smeared with blood from the fight with Iron Knife, the purpling mark of the blow that had stopped him from killing them all, Gunn looked like something out of a painter's vision of hell. His lips were thin, drawn back against his teeth, and his eyes blazed with a feral light.

'You ever do that again and I'll kill you.'

Abrams had heard men make the same threat more times

than he could remember. Now, he believed it, and it cooled the sweat along his spine like ice water poured down his back.

He watched Gunn walk to the door and stare out over the desert.

'They're too far gone. You won't catch them.' He didn't believe it himself.

'No,' Gunn shook his head, still staring away into the emptiness. 'I'll find them. One day. I made a promise.'

'So did I,' murmured Abrams. 'I said I'd look at your story again. Guess you can take it as read that I'll put in a good report.'

Gunn was reloading his Colt as the Texas Ranger spoke. He made no sign to indicate that he was even listening. As Abrams went on, he picked up a Winchester and a box of cartridges, began to shove the long, ugly-looking shells into the loading gate.

'I reckon you'll get a pardon.' The Ranger wondered why he bothered to say it: Gunn obviously didn't care one way or the other. 'When I get back to Abilene. I'll tell them what you done to stop the Comanch' war. How you brought the Dalton woman out. It should get you off the murder charge.'

'Yeah,' said Gunn. 'You comin' with me?'

He didn't bother waiting for a reply, just set off into the desert. The Winchester was cradled in his right arm and a water bottle slung over his left shoulder. He didn't look back as he walked away.

'How the hell you gonna catch up with 'em?' Abrams shouted.

'Walk,' said Gunn, 'until I find a horse.'

'Oh, shit,' mumbled the Texas Ranger. And started after the halfbreed.

They found Eleanor Dalton nine miles out into the Staked Plains. They knew her by her dress and what was left of her blonde hair. A good deal of it was gone in the shotgun blast that took her face, and most of her head away. What was left was thick with flies, a blood-bloated coating of sleek bodies buzzing furiously around the raw wound that had once been a pretty face.

The tracks leading away from the corpse were clear to read: they went south in the direction of the Mexican border.

They went down towards Pecos and Rattlesnake Springs, and it took Gunn another day before he found the stampeded horses from the Flying D.

By then they were out of water and getting mean. He caught one pony and they rode double until they spotted another, cropping dried-out grass along a low ridge. Gunn left Abrams under a saguaro and went out to catch the animal.

It was the roan he had bought back in Houston, and it came to him like an old friend, nuzzling his face when he approached it as though it welcomed his sudden arrival out of the empty desert. It still wore his saddle and he climbed onto it, adjusting his weight to the now unfamiliar contours of leather and stirrups.

The canteen was half full, and he dribbled the tepid water between Abrams parched and cracking lips. Then they started back to Abilene.

A day later the trail divided. Abilene lay to the south and west; the marks of Nolan and Christie's trail went due south into Mexico.

Gunn reined in his horse and tossed what little was left of the water to Abrams. The Texas Ranger caught the near-empty bottle and re-arranged his sun-baked face into a smile.

'You'll be headin' south?'

Gunn nodded.

'Like I told you, I got two men to kill. There's no other way.'

Abrams didn't say anything, just turned his pony off towards Abilene and settled into the pad saddle.

He was almost out of sight when he turned and shouted back.

'Hey, Gunn!' Azul could only just make out the grin on the Texas Ranger's face. 'I forgot to tell you. My wife's the daughter o' Roy Bean. I'll get that murder charge cleared soon as I get back.'

Matthew Gunn raised his right hand in salute and watched Abrams ride away to the east.

Over there, beyond the Staked Plains, off to the Missouri and the Mississippi, were the lands his father had told him about. The farm-rich, the cotton-rich, the wheat-rich lands.

Westwards and northwards were the cattle kingdoms.

Between were the First People: the Apache, the Comanche, the Sioux, the Kiowa and the Cheyenne; the Zuni and the Arapaho; the Pueblo and the Yaqui. Gunn turned his horse, wondering which world he really belonged to: the red or the white; it was hard to decide.

His father had left him a white conscience; his mother, an Apache upbringing. His heart screamed out for vengeance. But the two men who remained from the first long, lonely vengeance trail were still alive, gone into the lonely fastnesses of the southern deserts.

The trail pointed south and west, and Matthew Gunn, who was also known as Azul, went in that direction. He rode down through Texas towards Eagle Springs, and turned westwards, and north when word had it that the dark *yanqui* and the fair Southerner were headed for the Santa Rita mines of New Mexico.

He followed after them, waiting to catch up, when he would kill them. And fulfil his promise.

More books in the Series

HANG ANGEL

Frederick H. Christian

Angel rode into a town run by a trio of crooks and tried to help a hotheaded kid out of trouble. Within twenty-four hours he was listening to a broken-down judge telling them to take the kid out and hang him and, while they were at it, to hang Angel.

0 7221 6416 5 35p

HUNT ANGEL

Frederick H. Christian

When the Flying H boys hit, Angel found himself backing a town marshal with a busted gun-hand and a deputy with a bad case of the shakes. The word was out: hunt Angel out of his hole and then kill him!

0 7221 6423 8 45p

More books in the Series

TAKE ANGEL

Frederick H. Christian

The renegade fat man and his killers had done the impossible – stopped the Freedom Train and demanded $250,000 for the return of its contents. When they killed Bob Little as casually as they squashed a bug, they had Angel on their trail.

0 7221 6424 6 50p

STOP ANGEL

Frederick H. Christian

Ernie Hecatt was a cold killer. He was a rich and powerful man in Texas – until Angel put him away for ten years. His hatred festering in the prison cell, Hecatt plotted his merciless revenge. Three years later they met in the Valley of Death . . .

07221 6421 1 50p